FEISENGRAD

A SOCIAL NOVEL

Book I

Aaron Richard Golub

For Darrow

CONTENTS

MONDAY

Plausible Feisengrad found himself inside an egg on Monday. It slowly cracked and shattered as he pushed and picked his naked torso through its sticky yet brittle shell. With curly blond hair and eyelids sealed shut, his tiny potbelly form climbed hand over hand down a ropey cord that felt like an umbilical and landed flat-footed in The Z, where seven consecutive days were called a week and no one was safe, spiritual, perfect, knowledgeable, or good. This was his chance to live.

He heard a reverberating xylophone piped through burlap-muzzled speakers which distracted him from the pains and pangs of birth. He immediately sensed that this special noise called music, was pleasurable. Monday was known to be a day that caused anxiety and sharp pains. The Z Board would perform a full physical inspection and thorough investigation of him.

After moving him to a stainless steel room with fluorescent rails overhead at the Beefeater Hospital, they folded his arms across his chest while he was prepped. They slapped his muffin-sized butt, dipped him in pistol-cold alcohol, and exclaimed, "Clean," to one another.

"What difference will this bloke make, or does any bloke make a difference?" they murmured. The plow7s, who did what The Z Board told them to, were uncertain about their thoughts and decisions. Up to now, no one had made a difference, although the plow7s repeatedly muttered that someone would someday. There was a blind religious quality about that statement that no one doubted, because it was attributed to a catchall phrase called faith, that prevailed in the absence of common sense, logic, and foolproof evidence to the contrary.

When it came to the subject of the existence of a spiritual power, plow7s would say, "take that on faith," while others exclaimed, "take that up the ass" when angered.

Left on the freezing cold table, Feisengrad shook and twitched through the mystery of what was called birth; no plow7 in The Z ever knew how they materialized. After his blue eyes popped open, he looked around the room and exclaimed, "Look at dees. Look at dees place."

It was a strange place like all places.

Seconds later, the doors of the delivery room flew open. Two heavy-set orderlies wrapped a starched, white sheet around him, wheeled him out to a corridor and pushed on to the exit where a black delivery truck waited, its idling engine spreading gray exhaust through the dawn air. Feisengrad was shoveled into its cold, empty compartment. This was the atmosphere of The Z.

It was cool outside. As usual, there was trouble in The Z, and everyone was very worried; someone said this was spiritually connected to Feisengrad's arrival. Things were falling apart these days, as they possibly were in the very old days—no one knew for sure. This resulted in a phenomenon called confusion, which lead to other states of mind called consternation, fear, and anger. Meetings of The Z Board were instigated nearly every day to either take things apart or put them together; there was a meeting going on this very minute. These gatherings were held at a location called the Honky Tonk, a brassy building shaped like a trumpet, which was owned by The Z Board and was a place that seemed to have a political connection to cool music and well-designed sneakers. This wasn't true.

Following a healthy payoff to an honest hospital manager, the delivery truck dropped him at his parents' tiny, second floor tenement flat located at Egg Headquarters. It had a rear door, a porch, and a four-sided wooden, rotary clothesline. Feisengrad's father, Mr. Charles VDC (which stood for Very-Deeply-Caring), was an infantry soldier—dressed in a drab olive uniform, flat doughboy cap, and cocoa brown leather boots—on his way to the front lines at one of the Great Z Wars. His mother, Mrs. Esther VDC, was a housewife; that is, she was a wife in a house.

Charles and Esther VDC opened their door and wrapped their loving arms around the newborn. "This is the moment we've been waiting for," Mrs. VDC said. All the plow7s were waiting for that special moment, and when it occurred, they eagerly waited for another. Most plow7s experienced only one or two such moments in their lifetime.

This was a bad time. The Great Z Wars were necessary to keep The Z free so that plow7s could have fun without serving time in jail. These two plow7s, Charles and Esther VDC, were very excited about the delivery—their smile proved it. The really slick plow7s put on the Forever Smile, which required them to spread their lips to the maximum and show all their front teeth (which had to be white). A Forever Smile conveyed the message, "You like me right now, and I won't hurt you—for the time being." Moments later, Mr. VDC picked up Feisengrad who had been staring at and crying on the abstract linoleum floor. Charles VDC leaned into the screen door; its rusty hinges painfully creaked as they turned into the wintery daylight. Again, Feisengrad said to himself, "Look at dees place!"

The family descended the rickety wooden steps of Egg Headquarters and drove to the railroad station in an automobile shaped like a freshly picked carrot with electric windows. This was called a Moving Carrot and was manufactured and sold by The Z Board. Fueled by carrot juice, it accelerated when a carrot was suspended on a string in front of the driver. The VDC's Moving Carrot was given to Esther by her father in exchange for her promise to work in his bakery until the day a suitable husband was found for her.

Many plow7s of The Z drove Moving Carrots. Each one was a different size. The plow7s aggressively drove along Gold Street and the Speedway, cutting each other off, violating each other's driving space and causing accidents. This negligent behavior inspired drivers to flash one another the middle finger of their hand, a symbol that meant "up your ass," or "fuck you, asshole." No driver, no matter how full of road rage he was, wanted to put anything up the other person's ass or fuck the other person. It was purely an expression, and there were many expressions in The Z related to fucking plow7s or sticking items up their asses.

They silently drove on Gold Street and did not look towards the other three streets of The Z—Power Drive, the Speedway and Dirt Road. It was a long time since they thought about what they saw outside. Survival was on everyone's mind—imagination was a waste of precious time.

Plow7s thought about one thing more than anything else: the next event. On the way along Gold Street, Charles and Esther VDC did not notice that almost all the stores were permanently closed. FOR RENT signs either had been removed or were unreadable. They were severely weathered over more days than could be recalled by most plow7s of The Z who were predominantly shopkeepers.

Gold Street was made out of solid gold. It was an ironic trick, because no one on the street had any gold. In the most wretched weather, the dazzling luster and glitter of gold blinded the plow7s. On the other hand, it distracted them from the deep and penetrating agony their feet suffered when they walked on the precious metal. Stores or factories operated by plow7s were permitted to be open for business only on Gold Street. Plow7s were forbidden to carry on trade on any of the other three streets of The Z, but Umpires—who were elected by the plow7s and made up The Z Board along with the Cops—conducted commerce anywhere at anytime.

The ride to the railroad station did not take long; every building was close by. The platform was crowded with large and small families that had one or more sons or daughters drafted into the service of The Z. They stood around a tall bronze statue depicting the Falcon who ran an institution called The Institute. Many times, expensive statues were named after

unknown plow7s who were well-respected or known plow7s who were not respected. These children would be trained to kill the Enemy, whose identity changed constantly. Some plow7s said the Enemy was always the same group—their name, religion, and skin color was just switched out for different wars.

There were two Z religions endorsed by The Z Board, Coughism and Sneezeology, but some plow7s had their own. These plow7s were never heard from once they committed such a heretical act.

At the same time, the Enemy was planning to kill just as many or more of The Z's sons and daughters as possible; if they took prisoners, they would maim, torture or kill them. No one understood why prisoners were taken.

Charles VDC boarded the train and waved. Feisengrad would always remember his hand moving back and forth, the look in his father's hazel green eyes, the empty tracks, the station noise, the speck in the distance, and finally, all the families dispersing into a void. Everything had a beginning and an end, and plow7s excitedly looked forward to events that were seemingly over before they began. Time did not matter, as the end of war was as arbitrary as the beginning.

Feisengrad had a good memory; even if it deteriorated by the end of the week, it didn't matter, because it was all on tape. Esther VDC held young Feisengrad in her arms and cried for her husband's return even though he was absent for less than an instant.

Missing another plow7 was a custom in The Z. When a loved one (or even one who was unloved) was not present, he was missed; this caused emotional pain, suffering and wet drops called tears. Unstable plow7s in The Z, who did not know how to react to such adversity, demonstrated their distress by committing suicide.

SOME TIME LATER ON MONDAY.

Charles VDC, in his very pressed wool uniform, returned to Egg Headquarters and stood on crutches, his legs in plaster casts, at the bottom of its concrete steps, thinking, "How the hell will I get up there?" He cried out for help, but no one was around. He gradually made his way up to the back door of his second floor tenement apartment and opened the screen door. There was his son.

Feisengrad had been growing like a seed on a farm in a children's story, saying his first words, "Odey, odey, odey, duka, ducka, ducka." He did not recognize his father, who was badly wounded in the Great Z War. Now off the drum-beaten battlefield where carnivorous flags had gulped down innocent salutes, Charles VDC suffered from malaria, two broken legs, and shrapnel chunks laced throughout his body. Many of those embedded splinters and shards would twist, roll, and ooze from his flesh over his remaining life. When Feisengrad was older, a metal fragment fell from his father's face and landed on a dinner plate.

Feisengrad grew vertically and rapidly on Monday. Since his hands were large enough to play a musical instrument, he was introduced to a piano teacher who had a studio above a store on Gold Street. His parents dreamed that he would be a child protégé; the precise dream that all parents had in The Z. When Esther VDC worked in the bakery, she fantasized about playing all the musical instruments in an orchestra and singing the great opera arias for sold out, formally attired audiences. She imagined the plow7s endlessly praising her.

Her vision was that Feisengrad would be an artist—one who would get away with almost any type of aberrant behavior, because he had an artistic temperament. She imagined he would also be creative in speech, saying things such as "la, la, la," "baby, baby be good to me," "the wind, rain on my face," or "my dog is in the mountains." This concept allowed one to be respected for making noise, arts and crafts, and or writing down ordinary thoughts. Every time Feisengrad finished a piano lesson, his female teacher would award him with a white marble statue of a famous composer. He was very proud of his growing collection.

The piano teacher was hysterical and self-centered. She wore long, dark skirts, buttoned-up cardigan sweaters, glasses with black plastic frames, and red lipstick. In the midst of a lesson, she would break down into small mental fragments. She would inhale deeply, squeeze Feisengrad's tiny hands and push them against the keys, proclaiming "A flat, B sharp, and middle C, that is music. Do you understand?" He would answer, "Yes, I understand." One of the rules of living in The Z was to claim one understood when in fact one did not.

She wanted to teach Feisengrad a lesson. Plow7s of The Z would constantly try to teach each other life lessons. If something went wrong with the lesson and the plow7 failed to learn the teacher would always said, "I told you so," even it was a defective lesson.

Esther VDC came from a family of bakers, not bankers, who had worked hard in The Z. They wore white uniforms and worked in red brick buildings with built-in ovens located on Gold Street. They baked bread, cakes, pastries, and whipped frosting. One day, baked goods and pizza were canceled by The Z Board and replaced with vegetable, which was sold exclusively at the grocery store and Jason's Pizza Palace. It had four flavors that came from each part of The Z. There was northern vegetable, southern vegetable, eastern vegetable, and western vegetable. Southern vegetable was the tastiest. It was reminiscent of a bird called chicken, which hadn't been around for a long time. Vegetable had to be washed down because it came in the form of a plastic cassette that was swallowed through a deck-like mechanism plow7s had installed inside their mouths.

When Esther VDC was a young girl, her father carefully

explained that girls had to meet boys and get married, but she was busy in the bakery making bagels and glazed bread rings that plow7s sliced in half and smeared with cream cheese. These days, there was no cream cheese (or any other cheese) in The Z and no bagels.

It was so difficult for one plow7 to meet another plow7. Everyone kept to himself and was afraid to talk; once something was spoken, you were either on the air (where The Z Board would record what was said) or your words were printed in *The Ventilator*, The Z newspaper. The only way young Esther could meet a man was through a matchmaker, one who earned a living matching men and women for marriage. During this time, Charles VDC's mother hired a matchmaker who she dispatched to the other end of Gold Street to find a prospective bride.

Matchmaking was a multistep process. The first step was arranging a date—a date was an appointment with a girl. Charles VDC took Esther to a movie, which was a time killer that was substituted for blank periods filled with nothing to do. It was an activity where plow7s were not obligated to say anything. When plow7s were stuck and didn't know what to say or how to kill time, they would say out loud, "Let's go to a movie," and at the same time, they would say, "This is a royal waste of time," under their breath.

Movies were visual stories about Great Z Wars acted out by other plow7s who were highly respected for imitating plow7s.

They were called actors, and plow7s enjoyed watching actors pretend to be other plow7s. There were countless fictional movies made about Great Z Wars, and the plow7s could not tell the difference between a movie version of a Great Z War and a real Great Z War. That was how the word ridiculous came about because the soldiers who fought in the Great Z Wars imitated the actors, and the actors imitated the soldiers when they made movies. The Z Board had engaged in so many Great Z Wars and had made so many movies about the same subject that the plow7s couldn't tell whether there was a Great Z War or they were in a movie.

During the movie, Charles VDC didn't say anything. After the movie, Charles VDC was speechless. On the way back to Esther's tenement on Gold Street, she screamed, "Don't you have anything to say? You cannot be that quiet?! Are you doing this on purpose to raitz me?!" Raitz meant to irritate one to the highest possible degree. Charles VDC didn't answer. The following day, he proposed to her, and she excitedly accepted.

They were married early Monday morning, and before they knew it, Feisengrad was delivered. The Z was full of surprises; nothing expected ever happened. As a result of their marriage, the newlyweds had to move into a warehouse called Egg Headquarters, located directly above the grocery store operated by Charles VDC on Gold Street.

Egg Headquarters was a well-known tenement. All eggs were packed in boxes here by Feisengrad's two grandmothers and delivered throughout The Z via the Speedway. Plow7s did not eat eggs anymore, but they did scramble, poach, cook, fry, and boil them to ensure that they would not hatch any creatures that would threaten The Z's security.

The Speedway, which circled The Z and supposedly looked like a racetrack, was the only super road used exclusively for travel. No one knew who designed it; a detailed map of The Z existed but was never seen by plow7s who did not have the word map in their vocabulary. This map was kept on file at The Z Board, so Cops and Umpires could map things out.

Feisengrad got his first job working for his two grandmothers—Ida, Charles' mother, and Rose, Esther's

Egg Headquarters

mother—at Egg Headquarters; they hired him immediately as

soon as they noticed his little leathery body and nimble motor skills.

His hands were thick but flexible; he could pick up almost any object and manipulate it. While Esther VDC stayed in the next room and cried for the delivery of a baby girl, Feisengrad was cornered in the warehouse, living off the caresses of cardboard and the tepid warmth of eggs. The three of them weighed, packed and boxed eggs of all sizes (jumbo and extra-large) in a three-person assembly line.

Grandma Ida unfolded the grey and blue cartons, then Grandma Rose placed twelve eggs in each carton. Lastly, Feisengrad weighed the eggs, shut the lids, and stacked the cartons in columns of twelve. There were a total of 288 eggs placed in one large cardboard box for sale in the grocery below.

He learned that one responsibility leads to more responsibilities, and before one realized what was going on, one could unknowingly be doing the work of others. During Monday morning, Feisengrad was not allowed to leave the warehouse. There was trouble in The Z.

All of Feisengrad's relatives (uncles, aunts, and cousins) lived above Egg Headquarters in a tenement flat. His mother did not speak to any of them unless she had to. She said that they only lived nearby because there was no rent to pay, and the food supply was at the bottom of the steps in the grocery. Charles VDC took care of all his relatives who sat around like ladies at a sidewalk café complaining. It was part of the reason why he fought in The Z Wars—to keep The Z free so his relatives could eat. He was a good man who qualified to be called a very good man.

If Charles VDC observed another merchant overcharging a plow7, he would interrupt the transaction and explain to that customer that he was being "taken for a ride" when there was no transportation around. Dishonest merchants would angrily say to Charles, "You bastard! You did that right in the middle of my sale!" Charles would never call anyone a name, although there were countless pricks and assholes on Gold Street.

Feisengrad continued to work at Egg Headquarters. Jobs were hard to find and unemployment was always high. Some of the plow7s didn't want to work and would find excuses to escape any form of real labor. Their jobs ranged from singing songs or entertaining children, doing magic tricks or juggling wooden balls. Most of the reasons for not working were based upon medical conditions connected to depression or other psychological ailments.

Feisengrad was an exception. He was assiduous and would never be accused of laziness, but his grandmothers did not trust him and would follow him from room to room, pointing at him and making certain he was not lazy. Inside the grocery store, Feisengrad noticed that customers wore religious symbols around their necks or ring fingers.

There were two different symbols, a cross and a star. He discovered that the worship of God, who was neither seen nor heard, was permitted in The Z. This was a contradiction, as the word god was not contained in the plow7s' official vocabulary on Monday.

Coughism as well as Sneezeology had its own special god. Coughs wore chrome stars encrusted with shimmering small pink stones that said Believe. They were vilified and despised by Sneezes, who wore black steel crosses that were emblazoned with the word Faith. On occasional Mondays, Feisengrad's grandmothers permitted him to visit his father at the grocery on the condition that he promise that if he saw anyone who looked like a Sneeze, he would either run the other way or return immediately to Egg Headquarters.

The Z couldn't simply exist on its own, he thought. It had to come from somewhere, and that somewhere had to come from somewhere else that had to be made up by someone who made up that someone. This is where the term et cetera came from, and this could probably be traced all the way back to a god who couldn't be traced. Feisengrad figured out this theory inside the grocery store, where many questions would materialize on Monday—questions like: Is there a government inside The Z Board? Do they like a peppermint? Why do they lie to plow7s about everything?

Charles VDC worked the checkout in the grocery. Its customers—including winos, prostitutes, ex-convicts, bums, and pregnant women under the age of twelve—passed by his register. Almost all of them collected welfare from The

Z Board, which issued vegetable coupons to the plow7s. Charles VDC told Feisengrad that his customers were the most beautiful people (especially the women) in The Z, and he was so fortunate. In the old days, before the rest of food was canceled, coupons bought soup, white bread, penny candy, milk, and carbonated water. Cops and Umpires could get steak though which the plow7s knew nothing about. The only thing for sale in the grocery was the four varieties of vegetable.

Directly opposite Charles VDC's grocery store was a bar called Casa Blanca, which meant White House, but there wasn't anything pure about it. The building's exterior was made of inherently filthy, porous rock, which the owner, Jigger McGrail, kept painting white to hide its true color and distract plow7s from its activities there. Inside Casa Blanca was an endless poker game and loose women who wore transparent cotton dresses regardless of the weather. They danced with men, alone or with each other.

Jigger McGrail was a large, corpulent man. When one saw him, one would know him. He was famously corrupt, affable, cruel, and morally bankrupt, but a good family man. Besides, when one was tall, fat, and jolly, it added up to a good personality even though no one knew what was underneath. He had a lot of hair in his pockmarked nose, which was about the size of a C battery. Everyone loved him because he had a great sense of humor. He was connected to The Z Board like a plug in a wall socket.

Casa Blanca served two drinks: alcohol, which was 100 percent alcohol and beer, a foamy substance that contained a small percentage of alcohol. When plow7s drank alcohol, they aired out their political opinions. In these moments of intoxication, plow7s believed they were free to say anything, and they shot their mouths off.

Someone said that alcohol puts words in your mouth, and you have to be strong enough to take them out. Once in this altered condition, plow7s could do anything imaginable. If their actions were illegal, they blamed their behavior on the drink—they fired guns, crashed their Moving Carrots into other Moving Carrots, robbed, raped, vandalized, and murdered other plow7s. Such behavior was not tolerated in The Z. However, The Z Board permitted it with no regard to what The Z Board said about the benefits of recreational drinking.

Although Jigger had nothing to do with a quest for existence, he espoused his philosophy to his customers in a stentorian voice, "You should drink as much alcohol as you can to dilute the harshness of life in The Z and gamble every minute you're not drinking, because if you win a game of chance, you may be able to get out of The Z."

Some plow7s said that Casa Blanca was a façade for The Z Board's real offices and that Jigger was the head of The Z Board. Once a plow7 had those drinking and gambling qualities, he could go straight to the top, which was just a step below being a Cop or a member of The Z Board. A while back, The Z Board declared that the top was the really the bottom, and that it was nothing to get excited about for the time being.

Casa Blanca never closed. The women there would drink large quantities of alcohol, order fried chicken and boiled fish sandwiches—there was no fried chicken or sandwiches in The Z, but it sounded like the good old times to order them—and persuade men to purchase drinks. Men believed that if women consumed alcohol, they would allow themselves to be seduced. One could order anything in The Z, although orders were rarely filled.

By Monday of every week, every plow7 could be accounted for in The Z. The census was taken on Mondays, and Cops, carrying clipboards, entered every plow7's home demanding to know who or what lived there. Every plow7 knew there was no getting out of The Z no matter how much anyone won gambling at Casa Blanca, but they still tried.

But was a very important word to the plow7s. They used it to change or cancel the meaning of definite things they said and believed. For example, one plow7 would say, "This Monday morning, I was on my way to the Beefeater Hospital for a very important brain operation, but I felt better, so I returned to my room and went to bed." Or another would say, "I like you more than anyone in my family, but I'm not leaving you anything in my will," or "You're one of the best-looking people I have ever seen, but you're very short and fat." Butt meant ass, and butter was a greasy substance the plow7s used to spread on food in the old days, so it would smoothly slide down their gullets.

A little while later, Feisengrad was hired by his father to work in the grocery. There was only one other employee working in the store—a tall, curly-haired, flat-faced, muscular man named Dick Black. He had a small nose, long arms and was responsible for putting cans on the shelves in neat rows. Dick was the stock boy.

The cans were empty but used to contain sliced tomatoes, corn, chicken gumbo with rice, beans, and peas. Colorful labels displayed pictures of their former contents. Dick said to Feisengrad, "Never tell anyone what we do has no real purpose, because if you do, I'll be out of a job. Never allow anyone to make you fill out an application that calls for you to state your last name first. I find that insulting."

They stamped prices on the cans. The plow7s could buy a dozen cans of vegetable packed in two cardboard boxes called six packs. They hoped that someday, food would make a comeback, that The Z Board would replenish the empty cans at their food filling stations, which were now supposedly dormant. At this time on Monday, there was only the grocery, the first place where Feisengrad learned his ropes. Since his father gave him his second opportunity, and his grandmothers had first trained him as an apprentice, Feisengrad didn't have an official job yet.

Feisengrad's grandmothers waited on Gold Street for him. In the old days, there was a long real fruit and real vegetable stand in front of the grocery, and both grandmothers stood guard over the produce. They would say to each other, "The customers are wonderful. They support us, so pay no attention to them when they're drunk day and night. They mean well, even when they're mean." Now, the grocery displayed fake fruits and real vegetables on the stand outside just to show off. No one bought them anymore. Fake fruits and vegetables were commonly displayed in plow7's homes.

On early Monday, Feisengrad saw something he would never forget right in front of the grocery. His grandmothers screamed, and Charles VDC came running out of the grocery. A wino had stolen a fake eggplant and was dashing up Gold Street.

Within seconds, he was caught by a Cop and dragged by his hair all the way back to the front of their grocery. Charles VDC immediately recognized him as one of his oldest customers, a man who frequented Casa Blanca daily. He started toward the Cop to try to intervene, but it was way too late.

Trumpet notes sounded from the Honky Tonk, a brassy bowl-shaped building on Gold Street. Once a single note was played, there was no stopping the music. An odd but pure ritual took place instantly. An Umpire arrived wearing a dark blue suit, a chest protector and a face mask.

The Cop ordered the Wino to leap through the air and aim at a white spot on the ground called a base. Then the Umpire yelled, "OUT," after the Wino hit the base. Feisengrad would remember the Wino being branded with a large, black stamp that left an O mark, after he was called out.

The Honky Tonk

Baseball was not just a sport in The Z, it was a pastime. Cops patrolled the four streets and reported any plow7 who misbehaved. Then the game of baseball would kick in when it was time to call a plow7's behavior safe or out. There were no laws in The Z. Cops and The Z Board created the system, arbitrary rules set out in a paper rulebook; it cast a protective shield around the Cops and Umpires—the occupants of Power Drive. Plow7 after plow7 said he was "fucking screwed by the system" and would turn like a screw when they pondered the meaning of justice.

Charles VDC told himself that there was no point in explaining to Feisengrad that Umpires—an indeterminate number of whom were on The Z Board—attired themselves in the exact uniform worn by those who judged what was fair or foul, safe or out, ball or strike in the ancient game of baseball. It was a game played by rules, which always seemed to change. The Umpires carried the paper rulebook with them at all times but never consulted it.

All sanctions were imposed after the fact. No one was ever restrained from doing anything. Cops made subjective decisions about wrongdoing. If they thought, "Aha! This is a crime," then three things would happen immediately. They would 1) phone The Z Board, which 2) alerted the Honky Tonk, which then 3) blew the trumpet. An Umpire was then immediately dispatched to the troublesome area for a little game of baseball. A Cop was always present. Mischief threatened the order of the invisible system or invisible mischief threatened the order of the mischievous system.

The Umpire, dressed in a black suit, would arrive at the exact spot to render a ruling. First, he would place a white plate called a base on the ground; then, he would dust it off with a whisk broom, adjust his face mask, lift the bottom of his chest protector a few inches, bend his knees slightly and order the culprit to try to step or slide onto the plate. Everyone watching thought he or she was at a baseball game and was happy to be there. But it soon became apparent this was no game, even though the event was televised.

Since a Cop's pistol was trained on him, the accused always obeyed and headed straight for the plate. On the spot, the Umpire would call out one of two decisions and signal his finding—his thumb yanked backward over his shoulder for behavior that was OUT or arms crossed for behavior deemed SAFE. Since there was no ball in play, the effort to touch the base was only ceremonial. If the sign was SAFE, the Cop would let the plow7 go, but if he were out, the Cop would hold the plow7 while a huge stamp appeared and branded a large O on the back of the misbehaving plow7. It was a mark that could never be removed. Os were only allowed to speak to other Os, Cops, Umpires or winos.

The O Stamp

After watching the Wino being stamped, Charles recalled the image of his mother when she'd been mistaken for a thief. Those sad varicose-veined legs sliding for the white spot, the way she hooked the corner of the plate with the thick heel of her black laced-up granny boot and the way she was called SAFE, even though the crowd thundered, "BRAND HER! PRINT HER! PRINT HER!BRAND HER!" When Charles scraped his mother up off the ground, cleaned her up, and helped her back into Egg Headquarters, it was the most painful thought in his mind—more painful than his memories of the war.

Charles's mother, Ida, axed Feisengrad to come into the tiny kitchen next to the egg room. "I want to speak with you, so pretend you're a man," she said looking out the window on to Gold Street. She handed him a glass of hot water, stood behind a fabric-covered chair in front of the window and said, "Very soon, there'll be trouble for all Coughs in The Z, and they'll be given a hard time because of their religious faith." She stopped, retrieved her handkerchief from between her breasts and blew her nose into it. It was embroidered FEISENGRAD, SON, with blue and pink thread.

"The time has come for you to start a life career in the grocery, following in the footsteps of your father, Charles, and grandfather." She circled and gazed at him, "If you can be a success, you can change things." All plow7s, including Feisengrad, walked around The Z with boxes of hopes and plans in their heads. These were called dreams.

Feisengrad felt dismayed. He loved and hated groceries— that is, he would have loved to eat them but hated stocking fake ones on the shelves.

The piano books were put away, and the piano was sold because Feisengrad stopped playing.

Change was in the wind.

Everyone wanted change. Change this, change that, and change it all around. The truth of the matter was, nothing ever changed, and everything that supposedly changed was the same old change with the same name but called change—that was change in The Z. Feisengrad didn't know any of that stuff.

Feisengrad quit the grocery; he gave his notice and received a pink slip in return. The difference between quitting and being fired in The Z was always blurred. Feisengrad moved up Gold Street, and for the first time since he had been born, he felt free—free of eggs, pianos, and groceries. The first order of business in The Z was getting a real job, and he now knew working for his father did not count. He walked up Gold Street and saw a hinged wooden sign swaying in the wind outside of the Nylon Factory. It read:

OPPORTUNITIES AND ADVANCEMENT.
HELP WANTED. ENTER HERE.

He walked in to the Nylon Factory and applied for work. His application read: Plausible Feisengrad, born today. I played the piano, packed eggs, worked in a grocery as a stock boy. I went to the railroad station at the beginning of the last Great Z War, and I have parents.

Joe was the Foreman.

Joe was the most common name in The Z. It was a name derived from a plow7 who claimed he was the father of a god that plow7s worshipped. Many plow7s tried to feel as if they were god's fathers by adopting such a name.

Balling up the long paper application with one hand, Joe

pulled a short, fat, smoldering stogie from between his wallet-sized lips and bellowed, "I like you Feisengrad. You're a small guy with a lot of balls, and you'll go far in this job. You're hired. You'll be apprentice number one."

"Does that mean I have that several testicles? Does Joe have a lot of balls? How many balls do you need to go far?" Feisengrad wondered.

There was an upside at the factory for someone who wanted to get ahead. Feisengrad was anything but stupid, and he thought he could be in Joe's position some time on Monday. All plow7s believed that their ideas were unique, but in reality, other plow7s previously had the same ideas. Every factory employee wanted Joe's job, but they were never going to get it for two reasons. He was big, and they were small.

Feisengrad's ambitious aim was not to be on Monday because no one advanced quickly in The Z. A plow7 had to pay very severe dues before going near or far. This was another hard and fast rule of The Z Board. Rules, rules, rules. It was nice of Joe to like Feisengrad, and being liked was important, since that was the first step toward making a friend. Friends were key in The Z—hardly anyone had them.

The nylon at the factory (usually light brown in color) was made into thigh-length stockings for women. Women wore these items to attract men, as most men did not wear stockings, and it worked. Legs were one of the primary physical attributes of a woman. Men would say, "A good pair of legs turns me on," or

"Those legs get me hot." They would identify themselves as "a leg man." Such statements would give men momentary "peace of mind," and they would ax each other when they spoke of legs, "Have you had a good piece lately?"

The excess nylon was collected from under the machines, heaped into a baling machine—a four-sided steel box that compressed five hundred pounds of wasted nylon—and packed it into a burlap covered rectangle that was fastened with black metal bands. Then the bale, which was pulled from the machine with gaffing hooks, was transported down to the garage on a two-wheel hand truck.

Across the wide concrete floors of the factory, Joe and Feisengrad could be seen working hard, moving bales down to the garage where they were loaded onto a truck. Following behind Joe, Feisengrad walked through a room where machines with knife-sharp rotary blades were lined up like classroom desks; these machines cut the nylon strands. Female workers called operators, whose haggard faces looked as if they had lost the fight of life, ran each machine.

"They don't need a work break," Joe explained. "They're already asleep." Just then, operator number six screamed. Machine number six had snagged four of her fingers and sliced them off. The fingers dropped to the concrete floor forming a crumpled spider. Feisengrad went to help her, but Joe's arm prevented him. "Stay out of this. She'll be taken care of," Joe explained.

After she was removed from the cutting room, and the blood was mopped up, the factory owner emerged from a glass-enclosed office where all the job applications were kept on file. He announced to everyone at the factory, "This happens all the time. It's governed by The Z rule book. She'll receive four hundred Sanmarcos for each finger. She did not lose her thumb. It's fair."

Sanmarcos were The Z currency created by Louie Sanmarco. He was pictured on billboards moving in circles. No one knew whether that image was intended to show that Louie moved in the right circles or screwed a lot of plow7s in business. He was an Umpire now, but before, he could be seen frequently hanging around the square at the end of Gold Street, flipping baseball cards or tossing coins against a wall of the square.

Joe stood to the side, lying through his teeth, telling all the workers he was going to drink cola and eat sausage later, because he could get it in a place called the Black Market. He pretended to chew mouthfuls of sausage and swig cola from an empty bottle, while pointing two fingers toward the machines with rollers lined with hundreds of rows of steel teeth that crushed the nylon. "Every day, my boy comes out of there with two arms. No one else could do that."

The dangerous machines were housed in the back room of the factory. That was where Joe was pointing. Like huge prehistoric beasts trapped in mountainside caves, the machines agitated as their gigantic rollers meshed together, rotating as nylon was processed. Joe's "boy," Beauregard Dupree, worked on the machines, which he called "my babies."

Dupree was a heavyset man who walked as if a small creature lived inside his pants and was tickling him. His face was flat and sweaty and like the other employees he dressed in a green uniform during working hours but he never washed his shirt or pants; he smelled like rotted eggs. He fed the raw nylon to the hungry machines; he was the only one allowed near them. The only time the machines could be cleaned was when they were rotating. Dupree would risk losing his arms when he cleaned them, reaching up to the three rollers with two hand-sized, steel scrub brushes. After all the scrap threads were removed, the machines were switched off, and then he would emerge, his hands raised like a runner crossing a finish line shrieking, "I am the captain of the suicide squad!"

In the morning, during a vegetable break, Dupree would taunt the other workers while they waited in line to wash their hands. Dupree jabbed them in the ass with the broom handle axing "Did you ever take it in your head to make money?" When a worker answered no, Dupree announced, "This man sucks cock for free!" If the answer was yes, Dupree yelled, "So you are a professional cocksucker!"

Later Joe and Feisengrad were in the garage loading bales onto a trailer truck and pulling them inside with gaffing hooks. Dupree stood on the platform watching, increasingly angered by Feisengrad's quiet manner and unassuming willingness to learn the work.

"Watch this," Dupree said to Joe and muttered, "Small guys with balls...that's a lot of bullshit. Feisengrad, meet Beauregrad." He stepped onto the truck, pulled out his meat hook and pushed a nylon bale toward Feisengrad who barely got out of the way in time. The factory whistle blew over The Z, as it always did at this time of the day.

Dupree swiped at Feisengrad's face. Feisengrad ducked and fell back against the concrete platform, pushed back against the rocky, garage wall. As he slid down, his fingers scraped the floor; finding a broken bottle, he grabbed it. Then he taunted Dupree, waving it back and forth like a metronome. The machines stopped running, and the workers gathered behind Joe. He held the crowd back with his arms spread wide, while Dupree screamed at Feisengrad, "Did you ever take it in your head to make money?" backing him into a corner.

Dupree knocked the bottle to the ground and Feisengrad kneed him in the balls. Gasping and clutching his groin, Dupree twisted, reeled against the stonewall, then, like a lowered gangplank, fell flat on his face. He lay unconscious on the floor, his green uniform heaved under a swarm of flies.

Moments later, Feisengrad was handed a pink slip and was fired for insubordination. Joe said, "Your papers will be placed on file with The Z Board as part of your record. A copy will be kept for you at the Honky Tonk. There will be a ruling on your employment here, and for the time being, you'll be known as 'IDLE'."

Feisengrad went out to Gold Street and waited for a bus. In an effort to stop his hands from trembling, he made fists and put them in his pockets; he watched the afternoon traffic, trying to regain the composure he had when he worked at the grocery. No bus arrived, just a long line of Moving Carrots. The bus never showed, so he walked. About halfway down the street, he found himself in front of Casa Blanca.

Men inside were drinking beer. A man would never drink a single beer, because then he wouldn't be called a man, and if he was not a man, then he was a pussy or a faggot. No man could look at himself in a mirror and ax, "Am I a pussy or a faggot?" So, men would drink beer after beer until they were violently drunk.

At that point, they would fight until there was only one man left standing. The beaten man was taken out to Gold Street and left in the middle of the road to be run over by any random vehicle; then (alive or dead) he was called a pussy or a faggot anyway. This was the tradition at Casa Blanca, where losers were taught an important Z lesson, don't lose, but they couldn't help it. This bar was the last place Feisengrad wanted to end up after his encounter at the factory.

There was an alleyway next to Casa Blanca, and at first glance it appeared to be empty. It was a space where The Z Board allowed plow7s to sit to temporarily escape their creditors. Feisengrad saw what looked like a pile of wet laundry against the wall. Taking a closer look, he could see the outline of a person. Then, Feisengrad saw the face—it was the Wino he observed being imprinted in front of the grocery. The face peeked out from behind a thick, up-turned color of a tattered coat. There were holes in the knees of the Wino's pants, and they were rolled up over his shoes, which were tied with rope. A black ski cap was pulled down over his ears.

The Wino reached into his pocket and pulled out a bottle of alcohol. "I wish I had some of that wine that Cops and Umpires used to drink or cook with in those old gourmet meals, but this will keep me from freezing to death," he said grimly in a guttural tone that sounded as if he'd been gravely ill for a long time. He took another swig, pressed his coat sleeve to the side of his mouth to catch the excess alcohol and cried out, "What are you looking at?"

"I saw it all, and I can't understand why you were branded. What did you do wrong?" Feisengrad axed, as he approached the Wino.

"Why are you talking to me when you know you're not supposed to? You were a witness! Stand back!" the Wino snapped and went on.

"Wrong, there is no wrong except what The Z Board says is wrong. You steal from someone who's a crook because you're hungry, and you're punished. Tax is theft. You know where the money goes—to names, just names and laws passed by corrupt Umpires that have nothing to do with right and wrong—just what is good for The Z Board."

The Wino scratched his back against the wall and gulped some alcohol. "Wait, Feisengrad; wait for the next events. I only drink. I'm on a strict diet, because I know what they're feeding us. Vegetable control. The plow7s eat it, and it makes them say happy things. You know the expressions 'Do whatever you like' or 'Have a good time' or 'I'm a free spirit' or 'I am laughing so hard I could cry' or 'It's all up to you or me'?"

"No, I don't," said Feisengrad, scratching his head.

"They print that stuff on index cards at The Z Board then hand the cards out to plow7s and make them practice saying those expressions. You'll be saying that stuff soon."

"Doesn't sound that bad if it's true," replied Feisengrad.

"Oh, damnit! You will be like all the others. From the negative, you'll perceive positive. The idea that you can triumph is propaganda. Consistent defeat is the prelude to the victorious... Ahh! Simple math. The Umpires create these watchwords for every moment you live life. Trapped in those moments with words as partners. I got married, and I feel good. I am driving a new Moving Carrot, and I feel good. Tomorrow, I go on vacation, and I feel good. These words make you feel better, and where did these words come from? A machine! And where are they going? Into YOUR machine. It's Z control."

That was it. Nothing else was forthcoming from those wet lips. The Wino pulled his coat's collar over his face and turned his back on Feisengrad. The large, imposing O was between the two of them. Feisengrad made one more attempt to get the Wino's attention, a kind of friendly pendulum wave, and then he left. It was futile. He had no basis for understanding anything that the Wino said. Not a word.

Feisengrad was just living, moving from one event to another. The plow7, Umpires, Cops, what happened at the grocery, the factory, and the Wino... It was all too much to take in on Monday. The few short hours of Monday morning went by so fast, and as he would find out, the only thing he could do was wait. Maybe things would be clearer, different, later that day or on Tuesday.

LATE MONDAY

In the early afternoon, when the sun was directly overhead, Beauregard Dupree punched out at the factory and left for home. Since he lived in a tenement over a store on Gold Street, he didn't have far to go. He wondered if drinking at Casa Blanca the night before caused him to lose the fight with Feisengrad. Drinking all night was frequently the cause of fights. Too much of anything, even a good thing, was bad. No one ever explained why this occurred—it was just a rule that was followed. You better stop now because you are overdoing it!

When Beauregard opened the creaking door to number twenty, his room at the boarding house in the tenement, he thought about why his parents had given him a dog's name, and why he wasn't named Joe or even JoeJoe. Methodically, he pulled a new roll of duct tape from inside his loose-fitting canvas jacket, peeled off the clear wrapper and sat down on the wooden chair in his room. It was a good, strong, four-legged chair, and it had been there since he rented this room with a good, solid, wooden plank floor.

After he scanned the length and width of the wooden door and window, he stepped closer. Then he carefully taped the wooden window frame and door to keep air the out. There were a few more steps. The white dresser he'd had since he was Feisengrad's age was on the other side of the room, under a picture of wild flowers in a glass vase. With both hands, he dragged it across the room and pushed it flush against the door. Then he pulled the black paper shade down so there was no sunlight in the room. In the dark, his hands found the stove's gas jets. He dialed them clockwise to high.

Backing away from the hissing gas, he undressed and lay on the bed, curled up with fear and anger. His mind tossed around that one joke, did you ever take it in your head; he laughed quietly and breathed in the gas. His mind turned the joke over and over. He recalled the night before at Casa Blanca; he was holding a shot glass of alcohol and watching television, his hands on the highly varnished surface of the bar, staring down at his reflection, playing with a book of matches, lighting one after another. The sulfur smelled good was the last thing Dupree thought.

The landlady and her husband knocked on the door. The rent was due Sunday, but they didn't want to hound the tenants, so they waited until Monday to collect. Sunday was a religious day, and there was often a ceremony that occurred at the Institute. When there was no answer, they forced the door open. The landlady axed her husband, "Is Mr. Dupree dead, or is he sleeping?"

"I'll see if he has the rent money," she said while her wrinkled hand worked its way into Dupree's pant's pocket. His body fell off the bed and crashed to the floor. The landlady placed her fingers under Dupree's nose. Nothing there and no Sanmarcos in Dupree's pockets.

By this time, Feisengrad had returned home and was safe in bed watching television. This was no ordinary TV. It had no controls and was built into the wall opposite his bed. There was only one channel in The Z, which could only be turned off by The Z Board. It was called a set. The Z Board installed it early Monday morning right after Feisengrad was born. "You don't have to watch it, but there is always a beautiful baseball game on," Esther VDC told Feisengrad.

On TV, a thin batter wearing a red and white uniform was waiting for a tall pitcher dressed in pinstripes to throw a white ball. It would either be a strike or a ball. The pitch spun toward the plate. The batter swung and knocked it high into the outfield air. Another ball plow7 ran in a circle, caught the ball and threw it to a spot called home, where it crisply smacked into a round leather glove. A runner dressed in a dark blue business suit, white shirt and necktie charged toward the plate and slid hard into the catcher.

Plow7s normally wore clothes made out of thick, riveted denim called Riggs. It was hard to move fluidly in such stiff garments unless they were repeatedly washed and dried. They were the only every day clothes approved by The Z Board unless plow7s had a business engagement. In that case they were permitted to wear matching pants and jackets called suits, toping off their appearance with a fabric knotted around their necks.

The Umpire called the runner OUT. This telecast was played continuously until the viewer pressed a button that produced the following text: "I get the message." Once that threshold was reached, the television posed a question, "What are you doing right now?" to the viewer. One had to answer.

The plow7s curiously wanted the runner to be called out, stamped and ostracized. They were unsympathetic to their peers even though they could be called up next to slide toward the plate. All plow7s wanted something bad to happen to another plow7. It could be called envy or jealousy, but it was an inborn physical urge. The sliding plow7 usually had to suffer the misfortune of being called OUT.

Television was the place to universally witness equality, not real Z life. One plow7 after another could be called OUT, and rarely, if ever, was one called SAFE—this was equality. There was an endless supply of plow7s sliding toward the plate. Dirt and dust showered each plow7's feet, which appeared to protrude through the television screen into the plow7s' rooms. The Z Board had an insatiable appetite for taking plow7s out of the game as a means of keeping The Z pure, correct, equalized and wholesome.

Feisengrad had to admit to the TV that he wasn't doing anything, much less playing a game of baseball. Anytime anyone axed, "What are you doing?" the questioner was always doing something better. Were these images real or artificial? Was the question telecast to make him think his life was crap? He began to feel bad for the first time and acquired a popular condition in The Z called depression. The Z News came on next and a member of The Z Board made an announcement, "There will be transparent windows in The Z Board Building. Anyone can look inside and see what The Z Board is doing anytime day or night."

Weren't all windows transparent? If we see in there will we understand what those Umpires are doing? These were valid questions that no one was around to answer for him.

The announcement didn't say anything about what was being said or done at The Z Board, so Feisengrad thought there would be another announcement soon. The plow7s lived from one announcement to the next, not knowing why or how they were made. The number of The Z Board's announcements, which were usually but not always made at 6:00P.M. could also measure one's life. Charles VDC, for instance, was over five thousand announcements old.

Esther VDC entered the room and brought Feisengrad breakfast. "This is bread and butter," she said, failing to tell him it was cardboard bread and butter.

There was a knock on the door, and a copy of *The Ventilator* was left on the threshold. *The Ventilator* was not delivered; it was a newspaper blown over The Z by a large, industrial fan. Copies of the latest edition could be seen flying all over The Z following press time. Every plow7 received a copy on his or her doorstep. Everyone read it and said it was full of Z Board news. "This rag is not a newspaper," The Z Board said. "It is a philosophy. You can wipe your ass with it." What did that mean?

The Ventilator

At this time on Monday, *The Ventilator* printed an article

entitled RATES, stating that all rates and business indexes were up, adding that there was no method in place to check on the statement's validity. In The Z, plow7s and The Z Board announced and said many things about what happened, what was happening and what would happen. Plow7s had their own interpretation of the information that was disseminated, and they endlessly argued their points of view. When the Umpires observed these so-called "discussions," they felt satisfied when the plow7s were confused and wondered who was right and who was wrong.

The Ventilator was supposedly not owned or controlled by The Z Board; however, rumor had it that *The Ventilator* only reported secret information that The Z Board leaked to it. It was against the law for *The Ventilator* to have classified, secret Z Board information. The Umpires gave *The Ventilator* the nickname, The V. They would say to each other, "The Z tells The V what to report." The V claimed they had something called freedom of the press (given to them by The Z Board), but a plow7 who used to work there before he was imprinted with an O said that The V was only an advertising firm with one client—The Z Board.

Life was hard on Gold Street. It was important to pay the cheapest prices, but all businesses aimed to make a profit— business was business. Most plow7s immediately took advantage of the latest Monday announcement that things were up. They then opened their billfolds and purchased products that they dragged or drove back to their homes. Favorable economic forecasts changed everyone's lives and provoked plow7s to drink and talk about how much they hated life. That combination always led to fights.

Casa Blanca was never busier. Factory workers and women danced on the floor, on the bar, drank beer and said they were "plastered." There were so many fights—and fights within fights. An endless variety of fractured skulls and broken bones were commonplace. Jigger was raking in a large profit. "There will always be a winner and a loser," he said. "That's what God wants, and it will never be any different in The Z. I'm happy when there's fresh blood on the marble steps of Casa Blanca, the swirly kind right on the edge of Gold Street."

At the same time, Esther VDC returned to Egg Headquarters and went straight to see Feisengrad. She found him sleeping on the warehouse floor in a makeshift crib placed between piles of egg crates and said, "Little man, clean up and get prepared for the rest of the day."

He grabbed for the railing of the crib, stretched out, yawned, and rubbed his eyes. The sun, streaming through the tenement windows, spread a warm ray over his naked little body, and it reminded him of the many times he stood on this spot this Monday—just like the present—flanked by his grandmothers. They fastened a diaper around his waist, pulled on his trousers, put his arms through the sleeves of a blue wool sweater his mother knitted for him, and tied his shoes. He said "shoes," when they did this and nothing else.

Feisengrad turned toward the television screen and saw there was yet another baseball game. BASEBALL TIME was announced every hour. But baseball never had to be announced because it was on television nearly all the time. "There is nothing else to watch," he thought. "I have to worry all the time about being OUT." This time, the man in the blue suit was no longer wearing a necktie; he was only wearing a large O and was being escorted off the playing field. On the side of the field, the man, who's name was Jim, reported to a doctor who was wearing a long white coat and had a small, circular, mirror fixed to his forehead. There was a telephone number on the screen.

"So Jim, you tell me you're having shooting pains?" the doctor axed.

"Yes, Doctor, I have them shooting everywhere," Jim replied.

"Jim, you need to check into the Beefeater and let them do a full workup. Plow7s are dropping like flies. A workup is required. Report to the Beefeater. There are pills for every ailment."

The baseball game resumed, and men in blue suits took turns sliding into home plate. A burly Umpire called the plays from behind home plate and most of the men were called OUT.

Feisengrad dashed over to the pay telephone in the warehouse and called the number on the screen; a clerk answered at the drugstore, located on the square at the end of Gold Street.

"The Drugstore. We're located at the end of Gold Street, at Harrington Corner. May we assist you with your challenges today?" a clerk axed. The Square was named after Harrington, a past member of The Z Board. He was dead.

"There was an advertisement on television for the Beefeater. What is that?" axed Feisengrad.

"They give out our number, because if we can solve your problem with drugs, then you need not go to the Beefeater. We're a drugstore."

The Beefeater Hospital

"What's the Beefeater?" Feisengrad repeated. In The Z, one had to ax the same thing at least twice to be understood.

"It's the hospital where only ailments of the body are treated. Right now, we have a capsule in stock that can provide you with the thought that whatever is bothering you is someone else's problem. Can you handle it, or will you freak out, or may I help you with anything else?"

"I have never freaked out," Feisengrad answered.

"Wait, it is only Monday. Anyone can freak out at any time. You should get a dozen. The Z Board said that this would be a long week. Did you get their report?" the clerk replied.

"We don't have anything in stock, so you'll have to call back. There's a good possibility that there'll be a delivery later. One never knows, because the manufacturer consumes its own product. That clouds the availability. So let's have your order now."

Freaking out had nothing to do with being called a freak or the expression, "freak you, asshole!" When it happened to a plow7, he would act out of character, usually disoriented as a result of a loss. He would say and do things that he'd never done before, display weird facial expressions, hand gestures, and scream. Once a plow7 appeared to "freak out," his associates, family, and friends would no longer treat him as an equal. They would look down on him and think, "freak!" For example:

- If a plow7 purchased an item in a store, and he was overcharged, he would freak out.
- If someone slept with plow7's wife, the plow7 would freak out.
- If a plow7 wrote a story and another plow7 plagiarized it, the writer would freak out.

There were endless examples of freak-outs. The person who caused the freak-out was out of the equation once the victim commenced the freak-out. The rule was that freak-outs were bad but not necessarily a transgression that called for an Umpire to make a ruling. If the freaking plow7 freaked out in front of an Umpire or freaked more than once a week, then an Umpire made a ruling. The first thing anyone would say to the victim was, "Don't freak out!" or "Don't freak!" or "Don't freak on me!" but that rarely stopped the process.

Feisengrad hung up the phone, hit himself on the side of his head to see if he was still in The Z and walked into the white tiled bathroom where his mother was ironing her white apron. She washed his face, changed his diaper, and dressed him in a red long-sleeved shirt and dark blue pants.

Then he walked through Egg Headquarters and noticed that the stock of eggs was low, just a few eggs here and there; but this wasn't his problem. No one was working the boxes. From the other room that fronted Gold Street he heard sobbing.

Grandma's Death

Charles VDC met him in the doorway. "Feisengrad, I don't want you to see this," his father said. "Put your coat on and go outside."

Gazing between his father's legs, he could see the rest of the family sitting on wooden boxes. Grandma Ida was in bed. Ida looked at Feisengrad, and he knew she was starting to die. He looked into her watery crystal-blue eyes and saw all of her life experiences coming toward him on two tracks, one of sorrow and the other of joy. She was dying from heart disease. Death climbed up the tenement steps, slid under the door and skittered on its stomach across the floor of Egg Headquarters. Ida's head turned slowly as she raised herself from the mattress and put aside her pillow.

"Feisengrad, come to me."

He put his tiny hands on the bed thinking, "She has never looked more beautiful." Her lips were violet and around her soft neck hung a round onyx pendant; it was set with three letters that read SON. The first time she wore it was when her son, Charles, left for the last Great Z War. Her only other piece of jewelry was a ring.

"Feisengrad, I loved you from the moment you were born today. You are my favorite. Everything I own I am giving to you. It was made for you." Grandma Ida motioned for him to untie a knotted handkerchief she held in her hand. He lifted a small diamond ring from it and her eyes closed for the last time. Charles VDC wrapped his arms around his wife. Feisengrad cried. He had never been sad before.

It was cool outside. Although he wanted to go to Casa Blanca and have a drink or more than one drink, he didn't. Feisengrad returned to the grocery, went down to the basement and turned his face toward the black stone foundation. Feisengrad stayed there and wept until there were no more tears. The sadness was overpowering, driving him back onto Gold Street, where he stood straight as a ruler. It built inside him as if he were filled with tears. Standing on the sidewalk, he turned his face to the sky and said, "Please, God, I pray, take care of her." The sky did not answer. The purity of prayer lies in the absence of response.

There was no one around to explain what happened or what was going to happen. One was forever alone in The Z, Feisengrad realized. The death of Ida was a marker that measured life. Whenever anything changed, one was closer to death. Plow7s measured possible events against when death might occur. They said things to memorialize flying time. I must do this today. It is now or never. Today is a wonderful day. You must enjoy life now, and your health is everything. Time flies. I have no time left. Time did not fly. When Feisengrad thought about what occurred, he knew he was getting older, and like his parents, he, too, would eventually get married.

Feisengrad wanted to go to Casa Blanca and start drinking. Why not have a beer or some alcohol with some vegetable? No one would notice.

Peering through the open front door, he could see men and women who'd been drinking since early Monday morning, rotating on their wooden bar stools, watching baseball, pinching women's buttocks, saying, "Baby, you have a tight ass." This activity made Feisengrad think. Television was a plumbing system that was plugged into a sewerage plant on Gold Street, and the plow7s were being brainwashed with excrement so they would stay home and not make trouble in The Z.

After walking around Casa Blanca for a while without attracting attention, Feisengrad stumbled into an empty room next to the never-ending poker game and heard what was happening. Some of the plow7s had been playing in the poker game from the day it started way back when. Jigger was telling one of the plow7s who was fast asleep, "Playing cards is your life, and if you don't get a good hand, you lose. You're a damn loser, and it's hard to bluff when you're holding shit. And for every loser there's another one, like they were cloning the damn things. Thank God!"

Then Jigger dragged the losing plow7 by the shirt collar over to a pile of other plow7s who appeared to be asleep, drunk or unconscious. The loser would be immediately replaced. Another plow7 quickly sat down, put his Sanmarco chips on the table and began to look at his newly dealt hand. Afraid that Jigger might see him, Feisengrad backed up against a wall, which turned rapidly, delivering him to a dark space.

Was anyone there? An Umpire or two? Was it an abandoned building? There wasn't a sound. Not even a bug buzz or a creaking floorboard. He sucked in his stomach and held his breath. This was a crisis, and he had to figure out how he could get out right after getting in, like what plow7s felt about marriage.

A dim light was switched on, and Feisengrad could see things but they appeared fuzzy. The space looked like a men's club. The ceiling was painted with red and white stars and clouds. A huge whirring ceiling fan hung from the ceiling. The walls were red velvet, and there was a stairway leading from a landing to a gallery below that was lined with oil paintings of past Umpires.

There were marble columns sitting on large marble bases that towered over Feisengrad. "I must be in a temple, and there should be a prayer service honoring a God," he thought. Marble balustrades ran along the landing where there was a great landscape painting of places that did not exist in The Z.

As far as he knew, he would never see beautiful mountains and lakes. He wondered how such pictures were created, because no one in The Z had imagination.

It dawned on Feisengrad. This was The Z Board's meeting place, which was an area designated to make decisions about The Z. There was no other spot where anything that pertained to life in The Z could be used for that purpose. Every decision, including the serious ones, had to be made under these columns.

The Z Board

The floor was marked with an X where one was supposed to deliver a speech, and there was a sign, in very small print, that read, "Hold goblet aloft while talking. During war, toast to peace."

Umpires worked here, lived in mansions on Power Drive (as did the Cops) and drove Actolacs (The Z's other vehicle). The Actolac was a special car made for Cops and Umpires designed like a clear bubble on wheels. The driver could be seen from any angle acting rich and powerful and was admired for owning an Actolac. They were living large and were not making it a secret.

The plow7s were envious, a state of mind that made them desire what members of The Z Board had and what they would never get. The plow7s referred to this state of affairs as "the fat rat's ass of a chance." The Z Board labeled it the "persistence of inequality." They advertised that being equal was a virtue and the antithesis of individuality. Plow7s believed that lie while thriving on the belief that they were unique. On the other side of the room, there was a large gold sign that read, In God We Trust.

The electric fan's chrome blades turned at lightning speed and diffused a putrid smell. Feisengrad gagged, held his breath, gagged, and held his breath again, hoping to get used to the stench. When he was finally forced to inhale, he vomited uncontrollably on a painting of an Umpire.

"You see, this is where the shit hits the fan." It was a woman standing with one hand on the railing.

"Oh," Feisengrad answered.

"I am not going to ax you what you are doing here, Feisengrad. We have been expecting you. However, you arrived early. You were scheduled for later in the week." She was wearing a red dress and a black hat with a hoop brim, which partially obscured her face.

"It is now four o'clock, Mr. Feisengrad, on Monday, and soon the day will be coming to a close. You really haven't accomplished very much for a man who has been working so hard on the first day of the week," she stared at him. The only thing Feisengrad knew was that he was a boy trying to become a man, and four o'clock was the time of the day (symbolized by the descending sun) when it was too late to change what one had already set in motion. He backed up, tripped over a small red book, picked it up, quietly remarked, "Book," and perused it. There were many of these in The Z and each was supposed to espouse a moral.

"You are reading about my husband's life. There are pictures there, as well as a good story. Members of The Z Board always have their pictures taken, and they write at least one book about what they did in their life, even if they only lived a week." Stories about members of The Z Board were called biographies and were sold to the plow7s to distract them from independently thinking about The Z.

"My husband started in life as a dog catcher. Look at the

first chapter and see the color photographs of dogs. He caught more dogs than anyone ever thought there were loose in The Z, they wrote in *The Ventilator*. This accomplishment was widely praised because he started at the bottom, which is right below the top. When one does a job well that means success, and when one doesn't, that means failure.

"As soon as my husband was recognized for his talent, including his agility in snatching dogs off the streets of The Z, he was allowed to speak to plow7s about rights and a place called hell. When the plow7s became concerned that they might actually be living in hell or began to use expressions like, 'We're in a hell of a mess' or 'Hell no' or 'Go to hell,' he was made a member of The Z Board. Then he stopped using the word hell.

"He was invited to parties on Power Drive, we changed our last name to Lavish, and we were known as the Lavishes. We mailed out small paper cards saying the Lavishes are at home on such and such a date, which meant that you could come over for an icy alcohol cocktail if you were a member of The Z Board. I had to clean the sacred Umpire's uniform."

"You mean he called people's behavior safe and out? And he branded them?" Feisengrad axed and thought about his grandmother flying through the air toward the plate.

"I prefer imprint," she replied. "He mixed with the poor, and when he was not pictured in *The Ventilator* wearing the Umpire's suit or black tie (the Umpire's alternative suit of clothes), posing with other members of The Z Board, he could be found at Casa Blanca. The Z Board said he gave cash to plow7s to stop them from reporting him to the Cops for those photographs of him catching dogs. They were trick pictures, retouched, and reworked. Dogs were placed in nets that were never caught. He didn't catch any dogs (not a single one), and when it was discovered that dogs roamed free all over The Z, the jig was up.

"The Cops were called, and The Z Board sent one of the Umpires to the spot where he was standing. When he slid to the plate, he was called OUT. He was imprinted, and that was the end of his story. He couldn't bear to wear the O."

"What are you doing here?" he axed, dumbfounded by the ups and downs of her story that were clearly not depicted in the book.

"Oh, I am just the cleaning lady."

Then she disappeared. There were portraits of Umpires hanging on the wall. There were no paintings of women in The Z Board. Two of them were architects. A plaque said that they were hired by The Z Board to design space for the health and safety of the plow7s and to prevent power struggles. It was a system comprised of square, symmetrical buildings with corridors, elevators, and small rooms that kept the plow7s from massing into large groups.

Feisengrad wasn't told that these members of The Z Board were actually not elected because there were fixed elections.

Elections could be fixed the same way that broken appliances were fixed. The Umpires rose to prominence by the exercise of sheer power because they controlled a thing called responsibility and destroyed anyone who got in their way or spoke out against them.

They told the plow7s that they had to vote for candidates who claimed they were the best choice for the Umpire job. It was a lie. Choice was disconnected from morality and rationality, and choice never mattered because the candidates perpetuated the past problems.

During the so-called campaigns, the candidates pretended they were other people who were actually going to change things for the better. There was no such thing as better. Once elected, the person the plow7s voted into office seemed to vanish and be replaced by an exact replica that said things that no one had heard before the election, then things got worse.

Members of The Z Board figured out that there was no need to spend any Sanmarcos to get on The Z Board when violence or even the threat of violence could accomplish the same purpose. It was cheaper, paperless, and no one could prove anything about any member of The Z Board.

The Z Board said freedom is off limits because it only means that a crowd or an individual can only be free when rebelling, which never happened. They announced that any newly created constitution would be tantamount to moving in a full circle, back to the place of the beginning.

Umpires

Ultimately, any Z constitution and any Z list of rights suppressed expression because The Z Board would interpret it to their advantage or would delay making any interpretation until the plow7s forgot about what was to be interpreted. The Umpires were waging a war of the mind. They were eliminating their enemies, the dissidents and inventorying the souls of the plow7s in a catalogue that proclaimed the end of the individual in a fixed zero sum game. All this was exchanged for the security of The Z Board's protection from no discernible enemy.

Crossing Gold Street, Feisengrad returned to Egg Headquarters. He was always welcome. There was a brown straw mat outside the door that said so in large black letters. He wiped his feet and knocked, because he did not have a key. Charles VDC opened the door and embraced him. It was good to be home on Monday and away from The Z world. These walls will protect me, he thought for a second, and then he noticed that Esther VDC was packing.

"There is some good news, Feisengrad," his father said and stared at the floor. "We are moving to Dirt Road. We were on the waiting list and—"

The sound of a baby crying interrupted his father's words. "Yes, Feisengrad, you now have a sister. She is the required second child. She was delivered today, soon after you were born," his mother proudly announced.

There were identical houses called Opposite Houses on Dirt Road, where the land was divided into lots. So much of life in The Z used to be connected to rooms that were walled in square spaces that restricted movement. The more rooms a plow7 had, the more he was respected, and if a plow7 was living in what used to be called wide open spaces, he was called a hick, which was directly related to the word prick.

A plow7 was a prick if he was non-conforming; by living out there, he was surely an asocial prick. A hick was once an outcast in The Z at a time when there were wide-open spaces. No one really wanted to be in The Z, and no one really wanted to be out of it, much less a hick. So that is why The Z Board only allowed plow7s to live on Gold Street or Dirt Road, where all the rooms were accounted for and where hicks were eliminated. Everyone who lived in tenements on Gold Street dreamt about moving to an Opposite House on Dirt Road. It ran parallel to Gold Street.

There were four rooms to an Opposite House, which was directly opposite another identical house. What was opposite was the same. Dirt Road looked like reflections of two mirrors on opposite sides of the same object. No one had a dog or a cat. When the plow7s saw one another, they would say things like, "We are opposite, but things are the same."

Each Opposite House had a front and back porch and a shed to garage one Moving Carrot. Driveways separated the houses. The Opposite Houses were covered in fake brick called Brickola and had a small square patch of grass called a front lawn. An Opposite House approximated a square box, with two rooms downstairs—a kitchen and living room where the plow7s were supposed to live it up—and two sleeping rooms upstairs, one for parents and the other for their children. Plow7s constantly talked about their neighbors—that was called digging up dirt. The Z Board could use this dirt to attack a plow7 and that is why it was called Dirt Road.

The Z Bank, owned by The Z Board, gave plow7s a mortgage, a paper stating that the bank owned the house. Plow7s loved their Opposite Houses but spent most of their lives worrying about how to get their hands on the mortgage payment before it was due. When people turned their mortgage papers upside down, they saw that the letter Z was right side up. Z is Z no matter how you look at it.

Most of the plow7s read their mortgages upside down because the text made no difference either way; it distracted them from the painful thought that the mortgage payment was soon due. In sum, the proper interpretation of the papers meant that their house would soon be repossessed or foreclosed upon by The Z Bank. Documents issued by The Z Board called legal documents, were impossible to comprehend; nevertheless, they were interpreted in favor of The Z Board.

Dirt Road was beautiful in a limited and transient way. Certain travel expressions originated here. When plow7s saw one another, they would say, "We don't know whether we are coming or going today." It was said that The Z Board planned it that way—to take people up, up, up, and get them high on owning a piece of The Z. Then it would smash them and their hopes and dreams to rubble when it came to time to foreclose.

Feisengrad appeared perplexed, and his father made a statement that would stay with Feisengrad for a long time. "Son, don't try to figure out whether the move is good or bad. Life is about moving, not staying still. Be smart, save your energy for other things that are wise."

But there was a precarious thing going on in Feisengrad's mind, and that could prove to be bad. He was thinking about the word bad. In The Z, everything, even objects for sale or that had been sold, had a label attached, which had one word printed on it—good or bad.

No matter what anyone said as a short or long diatribe, lecture or discourse, speech or a song, or no matter what one did, such as playing a sport, eating vegetable, kicking a ball or staring at a clock, such actions would be judged as good or bad. Plow7s would say anytime, even in their sleep, this is good or this is bad or this is good or this is bad. They would argue with the labels on the objects. "No, this is good, not bad." They would argue with another plow7 who said something was good when they thought it was bad. "Don't tell me, I know that is bad."

Some plow7s claimed that they couldn't tell the difference between good and bad because every time they thought something was good, they found that they were wrong. Some plow7s walked around The Z saying "good, good, good," while others said, "bad, bad, bad." Still others said, "good, bad, good, bad," more or less alternating their judgments. What one plow7 said was bad, another plow7 said the opposite, and so the Z Board said it was going to eliminate good and bad from The Z vocabulary. But it never did, because The Z Board said that would be bad; at the same time, it announced that enemies of The Z Board's enemies were friends of The Z Board. Members of The Z Board had no friends. That was bad.

When the move to Dirt Road was complete; Feisengrad's room was wallpapered and his toys taken out of the box. He looked out of the window, something he did from time to time. When one thought about life in The Z, one stared into space or out a window. He immediately noticed that the plow7s who lived there acted strangely alike. In cold weather, they wore thick black nylon parkas with hoods over their Riggs, stepped in front of their Opposite Houses, threw snowballs at their opposite neighbor then returned inside. When the weather was warm, they changed into skimpy white bathing suits, oiled their skin, lounged around on lounges made from coarse colored nylon fastened to aluminum frames and broiled.

"Things will be different here, and you will have to make friends with another boy your age who comes from a similar background," his mother warned while she was cooking up some southern vegetable in the kitchen for dinner. "Friends, friendly, friendship, you know what I mean?" she axed.

"No," he answered.

"It is a mutual helping of one another. A friend will be loyal to you and will respect you. A friend will not be jealous or competitive. Most importantly, a friend will be someone you can trust."

"Will my friend try to have sex with my wife?" Feisengrad axed, although he never had a wife.

She thought about things for a minute and responded, "I have heard that if you can't have intercourse with your best friend's wife then who can you have sex with? But I don't know if it is true because..."

"Because why?" Feisengrad excitedly axed.

"Because your father doesn't have any friends."

"Oh, I don't know what having sex means anyway. I just heard it mentioned in the nylon factory's men's room, but I would like to do it someday," he said and returned to his room.

A few minutes later, she opened the door to his room, wrapped her arms around him and said, "Feisengrad, you will go to meet Cromwell. He is home sick in bed, and I will give you some fresh southern vegetable to take to him. He lives five Opposite Houses down the Dirt Road. It is the best way to befriend anyone, give him or her something. Plow7s like that, and if you come empty handed... well..."

Cromwell wasn't unknown in The Z. Many plow7s said, "He's been around," when his name came up. They were not referring to a trip around the Speedway. Of course, Feisengrad's poor mother did not know much about the other plow7s on

Dirt Road. No one knew much about anyone else in The Z, although plow7s would say things like, "I know him well," or "I have known her since she was a kid," or "There is nothing you can tell me about her," or "I know her inside and out," or "I can read him like a book, on the other hand."

Plow7s always referred to the two hands in The Z. These hands were large enough to accommodate two different sides of any issue. On the other hand, plow7s would say, "I am in shock over what he did. My wonderful brother really was not full of rage, and on the other hand, he acted out of character when he killed his wife. It is as if I never met the man, and on the other hand, I have known him all of my life. That was a side of him that I never knew existed."

In short, the plow7s had no idea about any other plow7s' character. At any time one could be standing next to or related to a serial killer, on the other hand.

When Feisengrad called Cromwell, he discovered that he was not sick, and Cromwell failed to tell him that he had been around, stealing cars, having sex with girls, smoking cigarettes, using a switchblade knife, cheating at cards, beating up other plow7s, betting on cricket fights, swimming in the nude and using profanity.

"Meet me at the Marble Works, Feisie. Can I call you Feisie?" Cromwell axed.

This could be my first friend, Feisengrad thought, although it should have been clear that Cromwell was not a normal friend.

"I am supposed to bring you some southern vegetable.I heard from my mother that you're not feeling well."

"Fuck that shit, I don't southern veg. Just northern, which has a real kick," Cromwell laughed. It was one of the few times Feisengrad heard anyone laugh.

"What is the Marble Works?"

"You'll see. It's the only mental hospital in The Z. You won't be able to miss me because I will be with Joy, and she is fine, very fine. If you go outside and stand on your front porch and look up, you can see the building between Dirt Road and Gold Street. It has a round shape, like a large clear marble, and it's all glass. Just like the marbles you snap around in your room. You must have played with them a thousand times, and I don't mean your balls. You can see right into the Marble Works, you can see the patients going mad, floor-by-floor. Have you ever been to a mental hospital?"

"No. Just a physical hospital , the Beefeater, where I entered The Z. I don't have any marbles and will have a look at the Marble Works."

"I heard they played poker in the Marble Works with toasted raisin bread for cards when that was around, but since it was canceled, they just run around their glass rooms screaming, 'Let me out! I won't hurt anyone! I promise!' You will like Joy. She is skinny and has real nice tits or nice real tits that you can feel. Have you ever felt a bare tit?"

"A nice tit or a bare tit?"

"A bare one is a nice one."

"What are you talking about? Are they cold? I've heard the word shit but not tit. Are they similar?"

"Feisengrad, you have a lot to learn, and I'm going to show you what a real tit and a nipple is, so be ready with both hands. And remember, Joy is a very religious Sneeze. She's not supposed to have sex, so don't say anything about God. That'll fuck everything up, and neither one of us will get laid. We have to meet her at the Marble Works, because her brother is an inmate there, and just so you know, he went mad counting all the men she went to bed with, I mean screwed."

"My mother said I should meet you too, so I will."

In the early evening, they met on the grassy hill surrounding the Marble Works. Cromwell was taller than Feisengrad. He had a small bump halfway down his straight nose, dark hair, and a Forever Smile. He said hello to Feisengrad and pointed to Joy.

"This is Joy. I am going to fuck her in a few minutes. I'll show you exactly how that's done." Joy childishly tugged at the corner of her mouth with her finger and raised her eyebrows as if this was something she didn't care about, one way or the other.

The fading sunshine bounced off the Marble Works, illuminating the scrawny forest that grew around the hospital. In the midst of Monday's finale, Cromwell and Joy ritualistically pulled off her clothes as if they were on fire. She was a little taller than the two of them. Brown, stringy curls sprouted from her small head. She had a high waist, her nose was wide and small, and she has a slight chin cleft, reminding Feisengrad of the doorbell at the Nylon Factory. She was already ringing. Her neck and arms were long, her legs short, her pubic hairs long and as natty as the hair on her head, and she was boney.

It did not take Cromwell very long to remove his clothes and put them in a neat pile. He was wearing his Riggs and blue sneakers, as was Feisengrad.

Then he said to Feisengrad, "Now it is your turn to get naked." So Feisengrad removed his clothing and made another organized stack next to Cromwell's. When he turned around, Joy was running in a circle with Cromwell, so Feisengrad joined in.

"Are we having sex?" Feisengrad yelled out. That was a common question axed in The Z by experienced plow7s who

The Marble Works

had sex almost every day of the week.

Neither Joy nor Cromwell answered. Cromwell grabbed Joy by the back of her brown hair and pulled her to the grass. As she lay on her back, her skin looked religiously translucent against the wet, dark green grass. In that instant, it seemed like there were only two colors in The Z, white and green. He felt sorry for her. No person should be lying on the cold ground even if they were fucking.

Cromwell leapt on top of Joy, thrust his hard penis into her vagina and moved back and forth like a kid on a rocking horse.

"What are you doing?" she cried out, as if she didn't know.

"Humping! Humping you!" He roared and winked at Feisengrad standing next to them on bare, freezing feet, ignoring the dampness of the ground, the chill of the air, and saying over and over to himself, "Look at this! So this is it! This is sex, and this is how it is done..."

He recalled when he was a kid earlier in the day when he said, "Look at dees, look at dees." Then his mind went quiet. He had seen it but didn't understand until now. He was in the now and not the then for once.

Cromwell was no longer humping. He was pumping fast and furiously and underneath all of that fury, Joy looked bewildered and traumatized.

"Are you watching what I am doing, Feisengrad? Are you watching?" he yelled. He removed his tool abruptly, sprayed her stomach and breasts with sperm, trying to hold it steady as if it were an errant fire hose.

The creamy, hot liquid flowed, and she cupped her hand, placed it over her eyes and cried, because all the plow7s in The Z cried one time or another. There wasn't anything sad about this occasion, and this was not the first time for her.

"Your turn, Feisengrad. Don't worry. I won't tell my mother, and she won't tell yours," Cromwell said. Joy didn't move, and things seemed like they were in the bag if Feisengrad wanted to have a go. He didn't but he wanted to.

Her body began to tremble, and neither one of the boys knew whether it was Cromwell's fault or it was the weather. Nothing else happened, and the three of them got dressed and walked in the direction of Gold Street, passing several plow7s on the edge of the Marble Works grounds planting flowers. A drizzling rainstorm was underway, and it was dark out. The three of them went in different directions, but they were all headed for Dirt Road, where Feisengrad went to sleep on Monday night.

TUESDAY

In the morning, the Umpires conducted investigations and held hearings almost simultaneously. Many plow7s said that they were investigated after there was a hearing, and the evidence that was gathered was not used because no hearing followed. Other plow7s said that the case presented against them in the hearing was unsupported by any evidence because there had not been an investigation. The Z Board announced over a loudspeaker, "It makes no difference whether we hold a hearing first and investigate later, because you are guilty once we decide to have a hearing. There may not be a hearing, after all."

The Z Board had specific methods of incriminating a plow7. If a plow7 was alone when there was a crime on Gold Street, and the Cops wanted to pin that crime on that plow7, then the plow7 would have to have something called an alibi to avoid guilt. The plow7 could not have one of those alibis if he was alone. Alone equaled, "I cannot have an alibi." There was also evidence received based on something else called your word against mine. This allowed the Cops to create a 50 percent chance that a plow7 would be convicted of a crime; however, since the Cops and the Umpires worked together, lived on Power Drive and were friends, the chances of a plow7 winning his caseere reduced to less than one percent when the plow7's word was put against another plow7 who was favored by the Cops. When the hearing was finished, the loser was handed a paper that read, "Now go fight City Hall." There was neither a City Hall nor city nor hall, and no one could recall if there ever was one in The Z.

Terror dominated Gold Street. Even the old pigeons disappeared. It was called Terrible Tuesday. All the plow7s stayed right in front of their televisions, viewing the horror, and The Z Board counted the terrorized masses, listing them as viewers. The Cops took advantage of the widespread fear, hanging their cloaks on a higher hook. They upgraded their intimidating appearance, wearing shiny, dark glasses, with metal frames and thigh-length black leather boots in to which they tucked their wool trousers. They drove chrome motorcycles and stood around talking to one another on all four streets. The Cops said their uniforms were custom-made, and they could not be reasoned with if a plow7 was arrested.

Instead of reporting irregularities to The Z Board, waiting for the Honky Tonk to blow, and an Umpire to be sent out for a ruling, the Cops first blackjacked and then interrogated the suspected plow7. They would inform The Z Board that the plow7 was injured and unable to step or slide to the base. Of course, the suspect had been rendered senseless and couldn't walk—never mind engage in the ancient game of baseball to prove his innocence. It didn't matter; almost everyone called in to question was being called OUT so far this week.

Charles and Esther VDC wore white, painted all their opposite house walls white and brushed their teeth over and over again. Esther VDC constantly vacuumed the entire opposite house (including the ceilings) scrubbed the closet walls and cleaned in between Feisengrad's and his sister's toes first thing on Tuesday morning. They didn't want to have any trouble, so they created a good clean record.

The temperature of The Z ebbed. Feisengrad and many other plow7s returned to Gold Street. On the way he met the Wino.

"This is the last time I can see you. What do they call you, Feisie? You saw my O didn't you? Don't you know how much trouble you can get into for looking at it, never mind talking to, me? I am not supposed to speak to you."

"Why are you, then?" Feisengrad axed.

"Advice. That is why I am doing it. Giving it to you because I am not supposed to, and that is how I received the honorable O. Makes sense, doesn't it? Or do you think I am working undercover for The Z Board?"

"No. Did you receive an O for giving advice?"

"Yes, isn't that what I said? Then take a good look at what

I am going to show you, and remember what I am going to tell you, otherwise you will wind up just like me." Pulling his coat off and turning his back to Feisengrad, he moaned. The red-hot coals from the branding of the O were still embedded in his skin and burning like embers in a fireplace. The Wino swiveled around, and Feisengrad jumped backward toward a hopping sparrow behind him.

"Ah ha! No joke! You better get it. Women, that's number one. That's what you do. Even though they all give out what's called the pain in the ass or increase the ass pain that is already there, you have to have one," the Wino snarled. He shivered like a freezing, starved mongrel, handed Feisengrad a bottle of wine and gestured for him to drink up. It was empty, but it had a nice label, displaying a vineyard and a man with a wooden pitchfork that appeared to be drunk. Such a place was not in The Z.

"Friends, girls and jobs. Those are the terms. You will be judged for that and nothing else, and if you do anything wrong to get those things, then The Z Board or the Cops will crush you."

Feisengrad already understood the extreme difficulty of getting these items in The Z, especially since he had been fired at the Nylon Factory and had only one friend, Cromwell, who he met on Monday. "Was he a friend?" he axed himself. After all, he showed Feisengrad how to have sex, and no one else had done that.

"Do what I say, little Feisie, or you will be sorry. You will draw attention to yourself without these things, and if you have them, well, you'll pass unnoticed. You want to blend in. The more you stick out, the more you will be disliked in The Z. The higher the risk that The Z Board will come to get you, take you off the streets, and smooth out The Z. You will be hooked with an O. You will be finished, and you will think of nothing for the rest of your days except that O. You will be saying, 'Oh, my God! Oh shit!' or 'Fuck, how did this happen to me?'

"If you are lucky, they will put you in the Marble Works with your own kind, and you can all ax the same questions to yourself or to the others all day and night. I am lucky. I roam because they let me. Call me a Z Board-licensed dissident. It is an advantage because no one ever gets out of the Marble Works."

Was he telling the truth? Did he work for The Z Board as a decoy? Feisengrad didn't think of that? The important questions occurred to a plow7 well after an event, and then it was too late. One thing was certain, Feisengrad did not want to end up in the Marble Works, where the inmates claimed they were forced to listen to birds flapping their wings, echoes of pigeons' gurgles, squealing bats, and frighteningly loud screams of children playing on Dirt Road.

A cloud of steam rose from the street, and the Wino disappeared. The words remained in Feisengrad's head. "Girls, friends, and jobs. Get a girl... where? I am lucky to find out so early in the week," he thought. He needed advice about how all of that worked, and it had to work in a certain way in The Z, otherwise why would the Wino say it? The words blew across his mind like tumbleweed until they became part of every thought he had, including his fears—a package of them then rolled into little balls of wet paper labeled "free thoughts of anxiety," and they bounced around his brain and unraveled into long pieces of string that wound themselves into tight little knots.

"My ways will change, and I will become the perfect plow7. I will get a girl, friends, and a job again. There is no way that I will ever be an O," were Feisengrad's last thoughts before he decided that he would take the first step. It always includes moving from one place to another, and from where he was, he decided to go to Cromwell's house. This would make two days in a row that Feisengrad visited the same place. No doubt The Z Board was well aware of this consistent behavior.

When he arrived, Cromwell was just walking out the front door onto the porch.

"Feisengrad, just in time." He descended the steps and moved past Feisengrad as if it didn't matter whether or not he was there.

"Come with me. I have to meet a friend of mine at The Z Bowling Alley," he said. This was the second time in the two days that Feisengrad had been alive that he was told where to go by Cromwell. Was this going to be a further moral deterioration of his character or a learning experience? Or were those one and the same?

Continuing along Dirt Road, without turning to see if Feisengrad was following him, Cromwell talked incessantly, running his words together. "It willdo yougood. Tongueis important. He is a bigbusinessman aswellas an Umpire."

Feisengrad now had to run alongside Cromwell, who was walking very fast. He watched the transparent glint in Cromwell's eyes, sending the message, "My lips are lying." But it didn't matter to Feisengrad; he wanted something from the situation, and in that moment, he was being sucked into this part of life where he had to obtain the three things the Wino told him about.

He wanted to say, "slow down," or "wait a minute," so he could get on top of things that seemed be getting away from him. But all of that would have been useless. Cromwell wasn't about to slow anything down for him, and it was a straight out, pure lesson in survival that he wasn't going to experience at Egg Headquarters. This was the outside world and classic Z life. He could see that everything was easy for Cromwell and difficult for him. This was called a cinch, and he wanted to learn how to make a cinch.

They arrived at the bowling alley under Casa Blanca. Feisengrad heard the shuffling feet of the dancers and clinking glasses from above. Cromwell introduced him to Tongue, a short, bald, unhappy, and wide-faced man. He was clad in loose-fitting gray trousers, a gray V-neck sweater, and black oxford shoes; he wore a gold falcon ring that mirrored the falcon atop The Z Board. Those rings were sold on Gold Street. There was talk that there was a powerful Umpire called the Falcon, and he could have been Tongue. Feisengrad was immediately impressed with Tongue's intense expression. His lips were tightly pressed together, and he had thick, black horned-rimmed glasses.

Bowling was a recreation that plow7s could engage in without getting into trouble, or so The Z Board said when they authorized it as a game that plow7s could play in an enclosure that had no windows. Sticking two fingers and a thumb into three holes in a large plastic ball and heaving it down a wooden alley at ten objects called tenpins were the two elements of bowling. It was yet another game authorized by The Z Board based on the movement of a round object. A single pin was called a tenpin. Cops and Umpires didn't bowl because it was invented purely for the enjoyment of the plow7s; however, one Umpire built a bowling alley in his house because he was a man of the plow7s, he said.

The Z Board announced that bowling was a family sport, and on Tuesday nights, the plow7s were required to bowl in groups called leagues and seek the perfect 300 score. On that night Plow7s wore bowling clothes: short-sleeved, two-color shirts, two-color shoes with white laces, and two-color gabardine pants. Their shirts were emblazoned with the number 300 on both sleeves, and all the plow7s incessantly spoke about the number 300. Their balls were stored in bowling bags. If one were not dressed in this attire, one could not step onto the floor of the bowling alley. The best bowlers had necktie-length, curly black chest hair, thick forearms and haircuts that were shaped like scrub brushes. These men called their wives sweetie, sugar, candy pants, lollipops, toots, or honey.

The plow7s tried to get strikes. Knocking down a triangular rack of ten tenpins twelve times in a row was called a perfect game (300 pins bowled down). Plow7s were told that if they bowled a perfect game, then they could get out of The Z. No one ever bowled a perfect game so up to then there was only one bowling joke. If a plow7 were close to a perfect score, the next ball that rolled down the lane would wind up as a gutter ball. Plow7s said the bowling alley appeared to be crooked only at that point in the match, and at all other times, it seemed straight, which was somehow connected to three words: but, nevertheless or since.

Tongue smoked a cigarette. Cromwell also smoked one and he blew large smoke rings down the alley. Tongue was a member of The Z Board, and it was inexplicable that he was at The Z Bowling Alley. This was called an exception to the rule, which one could interpret to mean that the exception was the rule, and the rule was the exception.

"I am here to enjoy the game of bowling. I want to keep busy. What do I do?" Feisengrad axed the two boys as he heaved a ball down the lane with a thud, before it wound up in the gutter. Then he picked up another ball and stared at the tenpins for what seemed like an eternity but didn't look around for anyone to tell him how to bowl.

The bowling alley was full and bustling. Every lane was taken, and as far as the eye could see, everyone was wearing their bowling outfits, even Feisengrad, who managed to rent the clothes and shoes from the concession. He felt like a clown, but he felt good to be wearing the same things as everyone else in the bowling alley.

The workers from the Nylon Factory arrived along with other workers from Gold Street. They were drinking beer that Jigger had brought down to the bowling alley. The workers were bending the empty cans, throwing them into the trash baskets, imitating a game called basketball and talking boisterously to their wives about how high they were going to score. "Check this out!" they screamed repeatedly. This sport meant everything to the tenement dwellers, and they took great pride in their balls and ball cases. It gave rise to the status called cool.

If a plow7 was cool, he was respected for giving off an intangible attitude that was interpreted to mean that no one could touch or come close to that plow7's aura. Cool was supposed to come naturally to those who had it, and if a plow7 faked it, the cool plow7s knew right away. It was like seeing a woman on Gold Street, staring into her eyes and realizing that she doesn't want to sleep with you because you were fake cool.

She was real cool, and it had nothing to do with temperature, although she would be called frigid. Beside other things, cool was something that plow7s envied. They wanted to be cool all the time—they even wanted to look cool when they were sleeping, and no one saw them. Women wanted to be known for being cool around men, and men wanted to be called cool just for being around women.

No other objective sought in The Z had a higher ranking than cool. Plow7s would say, "Be cool," to each other frequently, but they knew that you couldn't be cool just like that, at the snap of your fingers. You could not manufacture or sell cool. Plow7s wanted to talk, walk, sing, dance, think, look, dress and move cool at parties and in sports. Whoever invented cool couldn't care less, because that Umpire wasn't going to let everyone or just anyone be cool.

All of the activity in the Bowling Alley made it impossible for Tongue to concentrate, and he threw one gutter ball after another. It was very frustrating for him, and he wanted to leave as soon as possible. Tongue invited Cromwell and Feisengrad to his house on Power Drive. They were having a thing called a party—select plow7s gathered with Cops and Umpires, and they danced, drank, and told everyone the next day that they had a good time.

"That is the way they are on Power Drive," Cromwell said to Feisengrad and pointed to Tongue. "They ax questions and never listen for or care about the answers. They use the word

busy, which means 'if you wait a long time, I will finally be done.' You have to wait for them to finish what they're doing before you can hang out with them, and they are always very busy. They never look at you when they are busy. You have to twiddle your thumbs and pace back and forth until they have time to spend with you. Now this is how you twiddle your thumbs." He showed Feisengrad how to do it.

Power Drive was the street that did not run parallel to any other street. It was not just a road. Was it in a place in the distance that seemed to wiggle back and forth from reality to fantasy faster than plow7s' brains worked?

Many plow7s thought it did not exist or that it was only a thing stuck in their minds like depression. Their thoughts or dreams or ideas of how to get there were a plague on their heads, made up of irritable phrases that came from other plow7s who claimed they knew how to get to Power Drive. Phrases like, "I am preoccupied today and cannot talk to you, but tomorrow is another day." That would be followed sometimes by, "There, there, now, now, you will get there someday, just play the game," or "You can get there from here but I don't know the way." They were not speaking of bowling, although it was a game that potentially could get a plow7 out of The Z if he became a master bowler. But that wouldn't land anyone on Power Drive. If one could get a 300 or if one only could get it. Get it? If one were to get out of The Z, where did one go? No one knew.

There was no road to Power Drive. Only Cops or Umpires lived there, sometimes called Power Drive People (PDPs), and only they knew how to get there. The path was a secret, and it changed from time to time, depending on the latest Z Board map, which never contained accurate geography of The Z. A line of fir trees and thick shrubs hid the street. A white picket fence with a tiny gate was erected behind the vegetation. The spot allowed a plow7 to peer inside to observe a slice of Power Drive life; it was like looking through a keyhole into a very small part of a large room. One could catch glimpses of PDPs in white clothes running around on dark green, grass tennis courts swinging racquets at balls, or PDPs on horseback wearing black helmets playing a game called polo or playing a game called croquet, which required wooden mallets and balls.

No one could see into way into Power Drive unless he lived there or was invited, and no one was usually invited. Umpires' behavior was opaque and arrogant, and there was nothing to do about that except give them proper respect.

The Z Board and the Cops lived in houses. These houses (or homes as they were also called) had varied architectural styles and each had twenty or more rooms. Each one was built on a thing called acres, which was an abundance of Z land. On the acres there were swimming pools, tennis courts, flower and vegetable (all four types) gardens, ponds, weeping trees of every variety known in The Z, horses, dogs, and birds. Power Drive People called their street PD, and they employed live-in maids, butlers, chauffeurs, cooks, gardeners, and caretakers.

These employees could never leave PD without the consent of a PDP; if they left without consent, they were instantly stamped with an O right at the borderline, where there was a 24 hour branding station. No one in The Z would ever believe that the employees had ever been to Power Drive even though they constantly spoke about PD after they were branded.

The Umpires and Cops enjoyed life every day of the week. They did not have problems; everything they touched had a cool, smooth surface and was kept so clean. Once an Umpire or a Cop made it to PD, he forgot just about everything that ever happened to him back in The Z.

Power Drive was a seemingly endless exurb, and it was impossible to determine its size. Everything one could see on that side of the tree line, up to the horizon, was considered Power Drive. No one could see farther than the horizon no matter how firm his belief in God was on any day of the week.

Some older maps of The Z—which were probably fakes—gave the impression that Power Drive was the same size as Dirt Road and Gold Street. Every time a Cop or an Umpire drove on Power Drive, he realized that if the maps were accurate, he'd have driven right off the sharp end of The Z, which meant he could go infinitely in any direction.

Tongue's house was full of appliances and furniture imported from places no one had ever seen or heard of in The Z. "Holy shit, where did he get all of this stuff?" the plow7s axed. They would be told either that it was technology or an antique. That answer would satisfy a plow7's curiosity or thirst for knowledge.

Tongue bought everything that Sanmarcos could buy, and no one could outspend him. He turned down The Z Bank when it offered to lend him five times the amount of Sanmarcos he had on deposit, informing them, "We don't need it. We are filthy rich." The Tongue family spent most of their time writing out checks and folding and unfolding their bank statements as if they were small accordions.

The Ventilator wrote about Tongue and said he was a winner, although he never won anything. He began selling pots and pans door-to-door on Gold Street. A frying pan was stuck in front of every housewife's face, and if Tongue could not get inside the tenement apartment, he pried the door opened with a frying pan or wedged his foot inside.

"Are you the lady of the house?" he'd ax in a low voice. The door would be pushed against her, and he was quickly inside, sailing into his pitch about why she had to own a roaster, a toaster, a pressure cooker, a double boiler, a casserole, and a poacher. None of that stuff was saleable in the vegetable age.

The job got to him when food was canceled. Traveling around The Z with a cookery load in two matching plaid suitcases, knocking on one Opposite House or tenement door after another, finally resulted in medical problems. His doctor gave him a prescription for tranquility pills called Tranks, and he stayed at home, stoned. All of his Sanmarcos that he had put away from the sales of pots and pans was invested in Tranks. He got in on the ground floor and became very rich, not just rich.

The pressure from The Z Board to behave properly was so intense that the plow7s ate these pills every time they thought they might do something wrong. They became lethargic; no one was reporting to work, which caused The Z Board to call an emergency session. It was declared that Tongue had to make another pill that would excite the plow7s about work and cause a feeling of compulsion, or The Z economy would die. Tongue put his chemists to work.

At long last, Tongue reported to The Z Board, "Everyone can get high or low now. We have to be concerned about the in between. Our drugs will alter personalities. Some of the plow7s will be withdrawn, obsessed, attached, hostile, friendly, very hostile, anxious, intense, absurdly carefree, panicky, immobilized, suicidal, depressed, and there is always despair.

"The moods are secondary to the pill, and plow7s will experience middle moods. Plow7s will switch back and forth between these moods and will experience countless sides of themselves. They may have double, triple, or even hundreds of personalities. They will feel strange, and in the future, they hopefully will all act alike. The plow7s will carry folded papers or plastic bottles full of these substances in their pockets.

"Some of the drugs were called blasting caps, dillies, good horse, gravel, moonrock, monster, blow, blizzard, everclear, sleighride, purple hearts, whacktabacky, truck drivers, stove tops, rope, easy lay, dice, eraser heads, double domes, witch, red bullets, and hairspray. You could just call them dope, and all of them could be combined with one another to get a plow7 toasted or roasted.

"Plow7s will say one the following phrases: 'I am gone,' 'gonzo,' 'zonked,' 'too loaded to move' and 'zapped.' When they are high, they will work, and when they are not, they won't. We will produce more ups than downs, so they will work most of the time."

The Z Board was satisfied. The plow7s would be capable of withstanding the pressure of authority up to a point, and The Z would function efficiently. Everyone was temporarily happy, but how long would that last?

Finally, Feisengrad arrived at Tongue's house, but he had no clue how he got there because the trip had so many tulips, trees, twists and turns that he could never figure it out. There were a lot of boys and girls who lived on Power Drive in Tongue's house seated on the couch in the family room. They smoked cigarettes, listened to music and continually axed one another, "Are you having a good time?"

It was cool outside. The girls danced together and snapped their fingers. "This is a snap," they said, as they moved their bodies to the beat of the music. They wore tight pants called jeans. These pants were made by The Z Board and were much cooler than Riggs. They were unavailable to the plow7s. Joe College, Joe Blow, and Joe Perfect were neighborhood boys from Gold Street whose fathers were plow7s, but once in a great while, they were permitted to be on Power Drive, never really knowing how they got there or why, because of the trees, twists, turns and inaccurate maps.

They were also Coughs, which meant that they constantly spoke about how much they were not worth and how much the Umpires were worth. Worth was the most used word in The Z.

The biggest of the Joes was Joe Perfect, who thought about girls' legs more than anything else. He was tall, fat and had a flat top haircut. He was perpetually trying to uncover a good dirty joke. Right then, he was telling Cromwell one about a penguin who was not able to have sex with a beautiful girl unless she was frigid. But Cromwell was not interested because he was thinking about the girls dancing in front of him.

Joe College wore a white cardigan sweater with a tattered

red knitted letter on it. He constantly spoke about his old school while frequently folding his hands. "I loved my first day in class, and I loved sports and going to the drugstore where I met so many nice students. I love to study, and what I really love to do is read... I hate my parents."

The third Joe, Joe Blow, was short, skinny had red hair and a face full of freckles. He always wore white sneakers. And he thought constantly about why he was called Joe Blow and why his parents didn't change their last name. It wasn't just his name that bothered him—he was envious of just about everyone he knew in The Z. If another plow7 had a girlfriend, Joe Blow wanted to know how he was able to get one. If another plow7 moved to Dirt Road, Joe Blow would ax everyone how that plow7 made the Sanmarcos to live there? The reasons behind how any material possession was obtained plagued Joe Blow. These three Joes would become Feisengrad's friends.

Feisengrad felt out of place. The music was growing louder—so loud, in fact, that he thought he could see the notes in the space above his head. It was giving him a headache. He wanted to make friends with these Joes and get one of those girls, but it wasn't going to be easy. And that was why plow7s received these headaches from someplace. No one was paying attention to Feisengrad; that was just the way plow7s were. Attention was a warm bath of an experience, and it made a plow7 feel good, but when he didn't get attention, he felt empty, cold and bad. Attention also meant having plow7s look at you and touch you.

Time was moving, and it was getting darker outside. Tuesday was drawing to an end, and Feisengrad had to do something. The girls were looking better than ever, and he realized that it was extra exciting to see them move from side-to-side instead of just standing in one spot. They rocked, lifting one leg at a time in time, shaking their asses, shimmying their shoulders, pursing their fat lips and keeping their eyes shut as they grooved to the music.

The music stopped abruptly. Maybe The Z Board shut it down. Things happened in The Z when they wanted to happen and music was shut off when it was really being enjoyed. One of the girls turned and looked at Feisengrad. It made him feel uncomfortable, which was inconsistent with the idea of receiving attention. Turtle-like, his head retracted between his shoulders and almost disappeared. He avoided having any eye contact with her. Before he could see or say anything, she walked over to him and extended her hand.

"Pretty girls can afford to be aggressive," she said. The words stroked the fret board of his heart. "I am Grot. What is your name?"

"What's my name, name, name...?"

He kept axing himself what his name was and the word grotesque, as in Grot, flashed once through his mind. "The word, what was it? Translate it, find it, make it up, but do something," he thought. It was only a sound he told himself,

Grot

and he almost made a noise or said the word noise. Nervousness seeped into the sinking ship he called himself, throttled his senses and shackled him to the floor. This sense called attraction fell through his diaphragm, slid down to his stomach and stayed there like an asphalt lump.

His tiny hand elevated to meet hers, and in the quiet of the next few moments, they held hands until she released her grasp. Not a good sign. An educated Forever Smile of a clever woman shuffled across her rose-colored lips. "She has pale skin, so pure...and her lips...I want to kiss her..." Feisengrad thought. He didn't recall for a split second that no one in his family went around generously giving out kisses, and he couldn't recall ever being kissed.

What is a kiss anyway? Isn't it someone's mouth against yours? He thought about all these ideas and put his mental fingerprints all over the cynical idea that a kiss was a meaningless act that he needed from her. Then he thought about her skin again and wanted to touch it, although there were do not touch signs all over her face and body. And what about those delicate hands? Wow! One of them was touching the nape of her neck, and her eyes were closed. Her long, dark hair had long curls and engulfed her upper body like a beautiful scarf. Her eyes opened slightly, and she watched each effect she had on him as they enveloped him one by one. Both of her hands moved smoothly across her thighs, and her hips swayed back and forth. "Rich girls look just like this," he nearly cried out as the music started up again.

It could have been the lyrics to the song, and maybe it was her voice, but he thought he heard her say "Won't you come to my house? I live at Sixty Power Drive, and when this is over I will be at home." And just like that she slipped away, backing off into the distance to the area where the rest of the girls were dancing. No one told him that it would be like this, but why should they have bothered? It was only Tuesday night, but time flew in The Z.

Cromwell rushed over and insisted on knowing what had occurred between Grot and Feisengrad.

"Let's go into another room."

"Why do we have to change rooms?" Feisengrad asked.

"That is the way it is done on PD. When someone wants to talk about women, he enters a different room, puts his hand over his mouth and looks at the floor. Certain rooms are used for one thing and other rooms are for another purpose."

"What room are we in now?"

"Not the right room to talk about Grot. This is a standard room and special subjects cannot be discussed here. We have to go now."

Cromwell and Feisengrad looked around the ceiling and floor of the room, nodded and walked into the next room.

"This is perfect," Cromwell hollered. Feisengrad could hardly hear him above the blare. The rest of the Joes flocked in and gathered around. In The Z, this is how matters involving girls or women mechanically worked. Once a plow7 had spoken with the opposite sex, the other plow7s needed to know what was said or if there was a thing called a vibe moving around. There was no apparent reason for this phenomenon, but there seemed to be a magnetic force at work that put plow7s in a need-to-know mode when any prospect of someone else having sex was even vaguely floating in the air.

"This Grot, I know all about her," Cromwell said, looking down at the floor and muttering in a cynical tone. "She is an artist, a painter of pictures…once you see a picture of something, you don't have to go there. Every time she speaks to a boy like you, she tells them she is one of those artists." Joe College moved closer, brushing uncomfortably up against Feisengrad, while Joe Blow tried to listen with one ear. Joe Perfect combed his hair and winked at the girls who were dancing very close to one another and moving their shoulders in the other room.

"What does it mean, this information you have on Grot?"

"Don't take what she tells you in a serious way because you will get hurt by her. No one can cause more trouble for you than a girl, you get that?"

"I don't get it."

What Cromwell was saying was only partially true. Grot wanted to be a serious artist, but she was a girl. She was off to a pretty good start, because she stayed at home making sketches of life on Power Drive. She even captured the vast landscape of her father's property with oil paints on canvas.

These works troubled Cops and Umpires, because they didn't want anyone reproducing their life or images of Power Drive. They were afraid that the images could find their way into the wrong hands or any hands for that matter.

Joe Perfect stepped in and gave Cromwell a look as if to say he knew more about Grot than he did.

"Cromwell, Feisengrad hasn't got a chance anyway, because her father would have him called out. On the other hand, if he's willing to risk the big O, he can go for it." The music was so loud no one was sure they heard exactly what was said.

Feisengrad thought about what he thought Joe Perfect was saying, and although he didn't know what the words sophisticated or untouchable meant, he was willing to go for Grot. He just had that urge.

Feisengrad could feel that something great was going on now that Mr. Perfect had joined the conversation. All of the boys were staring at Feisengrad with newfound respect. Was he a hero? Is this all it took? Moments before he had been invisible, and only seconds later, he had passed a primitive test without knowing he was undergoing one. These Joes were becoming his friends, and deep in his little balls, he felt that he was going to make Grot his girl.

All the Joes lined up and wrote their telephone numbers down for Feisengrad, and they acted as if they had just been introduced to the elder statesman of assmanship. Feisengrad was happy just before midnight on Tuesday.

"Your phone will be very busy," Cromwell advised him. "You will now be talking to your friends. They will want to gossip and constantly tell you things that are to be kept secret, in strict confidence. Of course, that will not be possible in The Z."

The Z Board was still investigating the fight at the Nylon Factory, and until the work was complete, Feisengrad would be worried. Not one of his friends knew about that incident, and he thought that if they did, they might cancel their friendship.

Grot had her Actolac parked outside Tongue's house, and she offered Feisengrad a ride over to her house. Of course, he had never been in one of these vehicles, and he had only heard about them through eavesdropping.

"I would like to drive you to my house, but I just realized that anyone from Dirt Road cannot ride in an Actolac. You have to drive a Moving Carrot, and you cannot drive one of those on Power Drive. It is forbidden. So you will have to walk over to my house," Grot said.

"Okay. You told me the address. It cannot be far."

"It will take you at least two hours to get there, because it is two houses from here."

Then she left Feisengrad standing there in the doorway of Tongue's house, and he soon began to walk in the direction of Sixty Power Drive.

She was correct. He finally arrived before midnight on Tuesday. All along the way, he was stopped periodically by a Cop and axed what he was doing on Power Drive; he was threatened with torture if he did not tell the truth. The Cop also gave him four tests—walk in straight line, stand on one foot, sing The Z anthem and balance a small coin on your nose for ten minutes. Everything he said to the Cop was countered with, "We don't believe a word you are saying. You are a liar." They kept grabbing Feisengrad's arms and pulling him around as if he was on wheels. Then, a Cop opened a metal cabinet that was hanging from a creosote-stained post and called The Z Board. The conversation was incomprehensible,

"We have a three forty here that was trying to commit a two thirty-four, but we employed the four sixty-seven technique. We have the suspect who may have been looking for the target on four forty-four rub a dub dub at the club."

The Cop looked at Feisengrad and said in a plangent voice, while sticking his warning finger in Feisengrad's face.

"You can go now."

"Why, what didn't I do?"

"You have friends, you used to have a job, and you might soon have a girlfriend...you better get a job and a girlfriend when the investigation is over." Then the Cop spun around and marched down Power Drive.

It took what seemed like forever for him to walk up the driveway of Sixty Power Drive. Weeping willow trees arched over the curvy road and made it difficult to see in the distance, although the driveway was lit by streetlights. Except for the wooded area around the Marble Works, he had not seen anything like this place.

No one told him about what he saw on Grot's front lawn. It was a large steak tree, and it was sizzling. He did not know what it was. Although he was momentarily fascinated by real meat hanging from a tree he was overcome with blind emotion. What's a steak compared to a hot babe? Every Cop and every Umpire had a steak tree, and they ate steak every day of the week. At the same time The Z Board made consistent announcements posted in *The Ventilator* that "Vegetable tastes great, eat it." And he grew up on vegetable.

There were three different varieties of steak trees: Porterhouse, Sirloin, and Filet Mignon. The steaks grew on branches and could only be seen in the daylight, but they broiled around the clock. The steaks at the top of the trees were well done, the ones in the lower branches were very rare to medium. Each steak had to picked by hand by a Cop or an Umpire otherwise it would not snap off the branch.

Grot did not tell him about steak or her brother. Yes, she had one of those older ones who watched over her. A large figure, he opened the door and glard at Feisengrad.

"You asshole!" He yelled in his face.

"What's an asshole?" Feisengrad axed.

"So you are here to see my sister, and you don't have any money. That's an asshole. Go in the other room and wait, and I will tell her the asshole is here." His question was not answered,

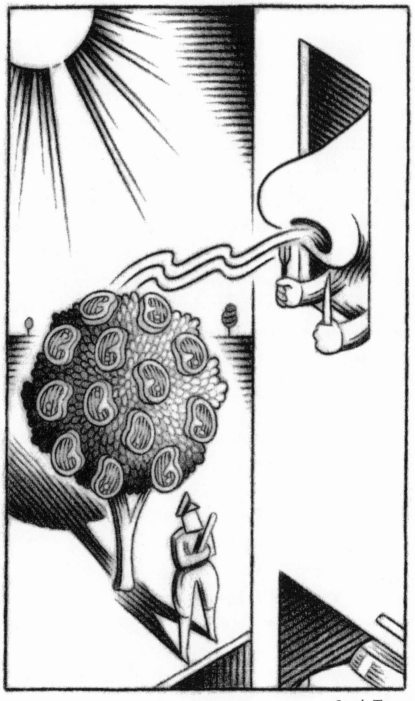

Steak Trees

and it turned over like a pig on a spit in his head countless times as he went into the next room; it was a living room where he hoped to meet up with Grot. Her brother looked as if he just engaged in an athletic contest, which required short hair, a thick neck, a clean face, gym trunks, and rubber-soled shoes.

With a white towel, he dabbed his sweaty forehead, wrapped it around his neck, looked down at Feisengrad, shook his head and looked up the steps that led to the second floor. Girls were usually on another floor when a boy came calling. Then her brother returned to the kitchen where he was just finishing up a nice, juicy Porterhouse.

While waiting for what seemed like forever, any plow7 would become restless, angry, dismayed and would get up to leave. The girl, in that precise moment, would descend the flight of steps and exclaim, "I'm sorry I'm late. I'm always late, and I hope you haven't been waiting long."

This was called a standard sentence or phrase in The Z. There were many others. Everyone on Power Drive used them, and the plow7s did as well. It was the best way to get through a negative situation, which plow7s created constantly, true to their downtrodden character.

Some other standard sentences were, "Please excuse me, I won't do that again," "I didn't mean to hurt you," "I'm sorry," "Please forgive me," "I apologize. I'm a human and make mistakes," or "Wow, was I that uncool?"

Some other standard phrases were "I apologize," "Didn't

mean it," or "Thank you." There were many more, and some plow7s said the entire Z language was nothing more than standard sentences and standard phrases.

"Grot, you better come down, because there is an asshole here to see you." He stared at Feisengrad.

"She will be right down."

But she didn't come right down, and it was almost midnight. It seemed like an eternity. Sure she'll be right down, right down, down, down, down. He was deep in thought about the word down, being an asshole, and how to get around being an asshole, although he didn't know what the word meant.

Was it the dark hole in the ass, which was really nothing, and if he were nothing, could he still be something—an asshole, for example? No, as far as he was concerned, nothing lower had ever been said to him. It just sounded low and down. "I never heard that word at the factory or on Gold Street or Casa Blanca," he thought.

All the confidence he gained from getting friends disintegrated. He had picked up some particles of confidence along the way that were rapidly dissipating, leaving him on the edge of a thing called depression.

And then there was the moment he had been waiting for. She finally descended in a sultry silk dress and lizard heels. He stood rigid in his Riggs, transfixed on this beautiful sight wanting to be loose as a goose but that was not to be.

"I consider this our first date," she said. He was about to

ax her if she only went out with assholes, but then quickly told himself that she must already know that, because her brother was her brother.

"I like you because you are not like me," she toyed around, uttering another choice standard sentence that Power Drive people used when they spoke to plow7s. "I could tell you were from Dirt Road, and you are real. I noticed that right away."

If it were Thursday or Friday and he had wised up, Feisengrad might have said to himself, "There she goes again with another standard sentence," but it was still only Tuesday, and he did not know shit from shineola.

What did like mean? I like you, and you are not like me? Was she saying she was like him, and he was not like her, but she liked him? If you liked someone was that like, like? Like, godamnit, like; toy, damnit, toy with me!

Did she mean she noticed he was from Dirt Road right away, or was she referring to his realness?

Not one of those things could be interpreted to mean Feisengrad was cool. If he didn't achieve that status, he could forget about Grot. As odd as Z life was, he found himself plunging further into the abyss of attraction—as if he were drowning at his first swimming lesson—the more she spoke about the things that didn't matter in anyone's life.

"Let's go down to my studio."

"Okay." But he'd never heard the word *studio* before because there were no rooms like those on Dirt Road or Gold

Street. Only PDPs had studios.

They went down a flight of steps to a room called a studio, where a PDP could make a racket or do arts and crafts.

"These are my paintings."

"What is a painting?"

"It's a picture, and I make it with a thing called paint, which is a colored, sticky liquid. Each painting is of a different fruit or vegetable, and that makes them valuable because there are no fruits or vegetables in The Z.

"Look at this canvas, isn't it beautiful?"

At first he didn't answer. "Can you explain what you mean by beautiful?"

"No. You either think it, or you don't. I will give you one example. I am beautiful." Now she trotted out a new toy—first it was art, and now it was beauty.

"I thought your name was Grot."

Then he opened up to her, told her all about Gold Street, recounting everything he'd been through since Monday—the struggle at Egg Headquarters, the Nylon Factory, how they finally arrived at Dirt Road, and the death of his grandmother.

"Anyone would think that it was strange and lonely," he thought, and she listened, giving his tale of woe rapt attention, or the same attention any girl from Power Drive might give. Maybe they were all nice girls from rich families... A long silence followed that made him squirm all over, although he was amazed that a girl like Grot could exude such sympathy and interest.

She must have walked along Gold Street, seen the tenements and cried. Her father must have told her about the difficult conditions at the Nylon Factory, how the Umpires and Cops had innocent plow7s branded. Maybe she cried. Maybe. What he didn't know was that Grot had been groomed to look sincere, and she was very good at it.

Life's natural rhyme and reason on Tuesday injected abstract emotions into Feisengrad's innocent mind, filling every spiral of his blond hair with the excitement of love at first sight.

"Feisengrad, we're so different. I just realized it, and I thought for a moment you could show me what I have missed. To go through that would be... be...be..."

She never finished that thought, but thoughts didn't have to be completed to get the message. And when one arrived at a moment of realization, that was the end of what the other person thought was a good thing, and that was the end of a good time.

"You don't understand beauty, and that is the most important thing to me."

Each of those words felt as if she applied it with an ice pick, and whatever good time he was having was turning into a bad time.

"There have been many things that have pleased me, but I never thought about whether they were beautiful, until I met you. There is no way I could feel the way I do if you weren't beautiful," he answered.

"You don't understand that I breathe the sweet air of Power Drive and not that stuff over where you live..." She rushed up the steps. Her brother showed Feisengrad the door and said, "I told you asshole."

Just like that, he was out the door. The understanding that doors open and close was beginning to slowly creep into his head as he walked back to Dirt Road with a broken heart.

The clock struck midnight, and that was the end of Tuesday. Feisengrad stepped onto Dirt Road. He did not sleep very well, but at least he had friends.

WEDNESDAY

In the early morning, Feisengrad sat on a wooden chair at the plastic kitchen table and had some tasty northern vegetable with Charlie VDC who was busy tabulating the meager earnings from the grocery. Feisengrad always sat to the right of his father. Even though the mood in The Z was upbeat on that Wednesday morning, there were slim pickings, because business was down. Plow7s were eating less vegetable.

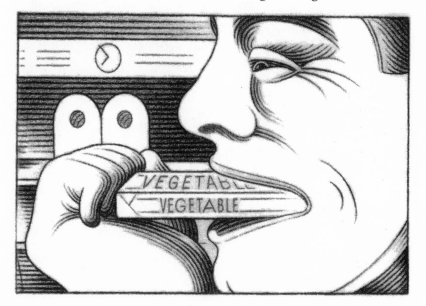

He recalled his state of mind on Monday, when he did not know the difference between red, black, and white. He learned quickly, not only about colors and shapes, but also about getting fucked around by a girl. He was a long way from calling everything he saw red a few days ago.

"Just give her a gold ring. You can buy one on Gold Street," Charlie VDC advised his son. "A simple gold band, just like the one I gave your mother. I never wore jewelry, and the only reason I wear this star is because I found it on Gold Street, and I hope, every day, that whoever lost it will see me wearing it, and I can give it back."

"Would a girl from Power Drive accept a ring from me? I have good feelings about her, but a ring...?" Feisengrad jerked his head backward as if he had been punched in the jaw.

This was sounding like a cold transaction to his inexperienced ears. He could not understand how one could go about giving a gold ring to someone—especially someone from Power Drive—who already had many things made out of gold, including gold teeth. PDPs were rich and tough. Grot might just take the gold ring and flush it down the toilet, or throw it in his face, or give it to her brother to melt down. The feeling of love was ironically, already, causing him deep pain, and he only met this Grot once.

The embarrassment of being turned down by Grot would be impossible to withstand in his delicate love-at-first-sight state. Feisengrad still had not fully grasped Grot's "get lost" message. get Would Charlie and Esther VDC have the time or willingness to pay attention to all the little bits and pieces of their son's story about this feeling of love? He doubted it, since they immediately skipped to the gold ring part. "Is marriage a transaction, a friendship, a relationship, a business, or all of these things?" he axed. Clearly, it was the thing to do.

Esther checked in with her two cents.

"Feelings? Power Drive has nothing to do with feelings. Every one who lives there is a perfect match for someone else who lives there. It is Wednesday, and you have been around the house long enough. You tried to get a girlfriend, you have some friends, and you used to have a job, so now you have to get married. It is not permitted to be a bachelor in The Z."

Turning to his father for help, Feisengrad looked at Charlie VDC, who was counting away under his breath with his head down. He was stuck in a trap—either get married and get out of the house, or just get out of the house. "You have a choice," his mother said.

"You have to want the things in life you can never have. These objects are called things, because they cannot be identified by name until you get them. They are there so plow7s can try to get them. When you get them, then you don't have to try to get them anymore. These things—cars, art, stamps, antiques, shoes, toys—are floating around The Z. Some plow7s and members of The Z Board collect many things, and beside their regular name, they are called collectors. So you must now collect a woman, and you will learn to love her, and she will learn to love you," Esther snarled and returned to the sink to wash the dishes. In The Z, women always spoke about dishes, the objects they despised. "I have to wash the goddamned dishes;" "the dishes are filthy;" "I broke another dish;" "the sink is dirty and full of dishes;" "I wish I had a dishwasher;" "you do the fucking dishes, because I am tired;" "it is your turn tonight; put on the apron."

A good-looking female, for some reason, was called a dish, a tasty dish, a hot dish, or a juicy dish.

Wednesday, also called mid-week, was a strenuous day in The Z, and most of the plow7s claimed that by the middle of the week, they were under a gloomy sky of stress. Many of the plow7s didn't make it past Wednesday, as they were stressed out and could not continue. They went right back to Monday and started all over again.

Most of them were relaxing with heavy doses of alcohol, pills, and sex on this day. The key reason this day was so difficult was related to a phrase the plow7s liked called the turning point—now was the time for the plow7s to choose how they were going to get through The Z. Did they have the stamina and fortitude to work really hard at what The Z demanded, or were they unambitious, tired, uncompetitive, and moving toward what plow7s called the wayside (the side of the road), and therefore no longer on the road to success? This was that time of the week.

"Time to shit or get off the pot," Esther VDC said, looking up at the clock. It was an easy way of understanding two things, Wednesday and shitting.

In his mind, he kept picturing Grot's brother who really was a thorough asshole but Feisengrad didn't know that. Thoughts were taking up too much room in his tiny head and why think about assholes? He was not a large boy for his age—whatever that meant—because plow7s were always sizing each other up for different purposes. They assessed one another's looks, height, weight, noses, penises, women's breasts, bank accounts, and so much more. Things had to be sized so a plow7 could have a strong sense of what to be envious of and what a plow7 did not have to think about. For example, when he looked at his own penis or his wife's breasts, sizing occurred. At the same time, everything was a different size, which made sizing logical.

What was he doing anyway? It was basic! Find someone in The Z from your background and never try to step up in rank, size, or class. Plow7s are blacklisted in The Z, and they never can associate with Cops or Umpires except for what was called once in a while. A plow7 could catch a glimpse of Power Drive, because the Umpires and Cops desired to be seen from a distance. An Umpire once said, "We like to see, but we enjoy being seen more."

Feisengrad wanted in with Grot, and that wasn't because he was ambitious or avaricious—he was in love, and that excused all other types of bad behavior, even being an asshole.

It was still late Wednesday morning, and Feisengrad couldn't bear to engage in more dialogue with his mother over Grot. Without thinking things through clearly, he wandered down Dirt Road over to Gold Street and found himself standing in front of the bar at Casa Blanca. Bars were always the first resort during troubled times.

He tried to reach up to the bar to get a drink; he also wanted to purchase a pack of cigarettes, but he couldn't get anyone's attention. Jigger McGrail's booming voice was emanating from the back of the room. Feisengrad thought it best if Jigger didn't see him, because he might call a Cop, and the next thing you know, he might have to step or slide on a plate. Was he on the fringe of getting an O? The jukebox was playing a familiar song that he thought he heard on Monday. Its purple and yellow glow was meant to transcend pain, and it worked for a moment, as he watched the mechanical device change discs, moving like a peacock, fanning and folding its wings.

He walked on to Gold Street and headed away from the grocery. That was the last place he wanted to be right now. Before he knew it, he heard the Wino's sad voice coming from the alleyway. He turned and saw him.

"Here we go again," the Wino said. "I think I warned you. My role, in my wasted inebriated state of mind, is to try to make sense out of Z nonsense. So there you are, in a pickle of sadness." The Wino sat on a wooden box. It now seemed like an eternity since they had met.

"True. I am in a very lonely place, because I am in love with a girl named Grot. The anger I feel inside is like a volcano, and I keep looking up at the sky saying—"

"Allow me stop you at this point, as I have heard these stories too many times in The Z," the Wino interjected. "That is where the word repetitious came from. Nothing is more common than a broken romance. Why do you think I drink? Rhetorical question! Broken romances from here to the end of Gold Street and down Memory Lane in my alcohol-soaked brain. Grow up!"

"That is what I am doing. It is only Wednesday and—"

"No excuse. Half the week is shot."

Feisengrad stood square-footed on the sidewalk, squinted into the sun and screamed out, "Haven't I had enough? Had enough?"

"The sun will not answer you, and neither will God, because God doesn't accept questions. He does not hand out answers. That is why God is called God, and that is why plow7s are always stammering, 'goddamnit, goddamnit!' I personally have found that the real beauty of prayer is the absence of response. God appears in those prayer books because The Z Board typed God's name in there. Self persuasion is no persuasion."

"What do I do?"

"Ah hah! I like when plow7s ax me for advice, although I wouldn't exactly call this an office. Do-do-do you? Hmmm..."

"I don't want to become alcohol-dependent, and I don't

want to start to smoke," Feisengrad answered limply.

"That leaves God as a last choice. Yes, you don't want your clothes smelling like mine, not to mention the wet urine. Get a whiff of this." The Wino pointed to his crotch; his pants looked forever wet around the unbuttoned fly. "Yes, I pee in my pants, because there is no available toilet around here. You think that Jigger M. would ever let me use the john? Please don't answer that one. So I pee in my pants. It is very warm, but I am wet. This doesn't mean I don't know what I am talking about. You wait and see, The Z isn't just about the Umpires and Cops. There are plow7s out to get you, because you have it on wrong and your own are the worst kind."

Feisengrad looked at his severe hand-me-down shirt and pants and figured that they were on correctly, although his Riggs were baggy in the back, too long in the front, and the pockets were too short to put his hands in all the way.

"Who is out to get me?"

"The Sneezes?"

"Son Easys? Never heard of them."

"You better learn how to pronounce Sneezes, because they're gathering in the Square at the end of Gold Street, and they're getting angry. They were always mad about something. Over plow7s who don't look like them and don't have their whitey-white skin color and blondie-blond hair. Although some of them don't have blondie-blond hair, because they bleach it, and they aren't so whitey-white. The Sneezes want all the

Coughs to cut their hair in the shape of a Z, otherwise they will be killed."

"Huh?"

"Tonight is going to be a wicked one, and if I were you, I would stay off Gold Street, go back to Dirt Road, go into your room, get under the bed, and then get under the floorboards. Or go get a haircut and make certain it is in the shape of a Z," the Wino warned.

Feisengrad looked up at the sky as if the weather was going to turn any second.

"Should this be taken seriously?" he asked himself. The Wino was a sad, comedic, alcoholic, intelligent pariah who nevertheless existed, and that, in and of itself, was enough to give him credibility. One had to be circumspect in The Z, because outlandish behavior was very often accepted as just another part of The Z life, when, in fact, it was not.

When Feisengrad looked, the Wino had vanished. Just then, Joe Perfect pulled over in a new Moving Carrot and got out on the sidewalk. Joe's black hair was slicked back, his pants were tapered, and he wore black, pointed shoes. This appearance meant that this plow7 had a date with a girl.

"C'mon with me, Feisengrad, jump in. Midge is waiting for me, and I'm supposed to pick her up on Gold Street. She's standing in front of the Very Dry Cleaner. I brought her some flowers," he said proudly, knowing that Feisengrad knew how difficult it was to get a date in The Z.

The wives of Umpires and Cops sat in their gardens, growing flowers and eating little cakes made out of vegetable. They were cranking out small etiquette books dedicated to the way plow7s were supposed to behave, including how to act on a date in The Z. These tiny volumes were stored on every bookcase on Power Drive. They described plow7s' bad dating behavior with illustrations of them using the wrong verb, wrong knife, or wearing mismatched colors.

Joe presented himself as a wizard at fixing things (especially electronic gadgets) a talent of which he was very proud. Whenever anyone axed him how he was, he always responded, "Perfect." There wasn't a day when he wasn't without a pair of needle-nose pliers, talking about the fact that he could fix anything and make it perfect.

On any given day, he would approach any plow7 who had a mobile phone, camera, or radio on Gold Street and say, "Your phone is not working properly," or "Your radio is full of static, and I can make it sound better. Clearer." Then the plow7 would hand over the device, and he would pick it apart with his needle-nose pliers, reducing the valuable instrument to shreds. A bright, regular smile would break across Joe's face, and he would say, "Perfect." Once finished, Joe would hand over the dismantled device, together with its parts and wires, to the bewildered owner and say, "I think it will work better now. It is fixed." Then he would walk away.

"Feisengrad, I can fix anything that is broken, if it is

electronic, electric, or mechanical," he said, before they arrived at their destination. "Just think of me as your handyman and friend."

"Someone just told me that the Sneezes are going to kill all the Coughs who don't cut their hair in the shape of a Z. Did you hear that?"

"You're crazy," Joe replied.

A few minutes later, Joe Perfect and Feisengrad pulled up in front of the Very Dry Cleaner. Midge and her burly father stood there like statues. Feisengrad thought she was pretty and looked great in her orange dress and white shoes, but he immediately suppressed any other thoughts about Midge. He was not supposed to think about fucking his friend's girlfriend, especially when her father was present. Grot was still on his mind; however, this type of restraint was impossible. These girls always had large breasts and large fathers.

The Very Dry Cleaner was located right next to the drugstore in the Square, and its sign read VDC, which confused Feisengrad, since the letters of his parents' last name were the same. Joe took his foot off the Moving Carrot's accelerator and looked in the mirror. "Let's go and get Midge. She looks good."

"All right," Feisengrad agreed, although he had no idea what all right meant. He was still fixated on The Z Cut and couldn't picture Joe Perfect doing anything to a single hair on his greasy head, much less cutting it into a Z or any other letter or number.

They stepped onto the sidewalk and immediately noticed the way to the Very Dry Cleaner was blocked by eight plow7s called The Harrington Corner Boys. The Square had two corners because Gold Street stopped there. One corner was marked with raised concrete letters that read Harrington Corner; it was named after a dead Umpire called Harrington. Square and corners were always named after dead Umpires.

The Harrington Corner Boys were tough but not smart, although they prided themselves on sentences called wisecracks. Plow7s called them wiseguys. A wiseguy was not a man of wisdom but usually a man of power. In The Z, power always trumped wisdom. It was one thing to lose an intellectual argument, but it was far worse for plow7s to get their teeth punched out of their mouths or to suffer broken bones because of an interlude with a wisecracking wiseguy. They leaned against the concrete wall of the drugstore, elbowed each other in the ribs, rolled their sleeves up, rolled their sleeves down, made Forever Smiles, and morphed into beacons searching for trouble. They'd been waiting for plow7s like Feisengrad and Joe Perfect to enter Harrington Corner.

Wednesday was a day that these two plow7s should have stayed home. The Coughs were the Harrington Corner Boys' prey. Theirs was a religious war, not just the strong beating up on the weak. "What is the difference if there are more of them then us?" a Cough once axed. There were more

Sneezes than Coughs, and if a plow7 didn't have a Z cut, he was going down.

Every day, the Harrington Corner Boys repeatedly said to no one in particular, "We are going to beat the shit out of you." That's where the expression scared shitless originated, and it was what made the Coughs cough and the Sneezes tough. Sometimes, Coughs coughed up blood, and other times, it was vegetable. The Sneezes did not mean that literally, although getting totally rid of shit would be a strong step in the direction of achieving purity. They would also have to resolve the problem of using shit as fertilizer to grow vegetable and for the ingredients used in beer.

The Cops and Umpires never interfered, because The Z periodically needed to be cleansed of the Coughs. They were always multiplying in numbers, good at making Sanmarcos, good in business enterprises, kept to themselves, and supposedly had long noses. Noses in The Z came in all shapes and sizes. Even some of the Umpires had large noses with warts. There was more than one reason for the mask.

No one knew where all these Coughs came from; some Cops secretly said Coughs actually came from all over The Z or from outside The Z, and they were the chosen plow7s of the real God. Was that why they multiplied so quickly? Was it like thousands of bees hatched by the queen bee? Those characteristics made the Cops, Umpires, and the Harrington Corner Boys angry and envious.

The whole purpose of The Z was to keep it pure, although the only way for it to remain that way was to weed out the poisons and the vermin Coughs. If purity was a natural phenomenon, there would be nothing for the Sneezes to do to keep The Z pure. It stayed pure on its own except for the Coughs; the word except was similar to the word but.

The Z was not pure and never would be, so long as there were Coughs, so said the Sneezes. So, there always had to be a certain number of Coughs to eliminate to reach a level of imaginary purity, unless they adhered to the Harrington Corner Boys' mandate and got a Z cut on Wednesday.

The leader of the Harrington Corner Boys was Toastie Fusco, a pure Sneeze, who was tall, thin, and very strong. His wiry frame could make toast out of anyone—that was how he got his nickname; there had been no toast in The Z for a long time. No one understood the expression, "I am going to make toast out of you," because that process was impossible; however, the plow7s imagined that if Toastie kicked and punched a plow7, he would look more like toast than anything else. Plow7s accepted the idea that toast was black and blue and bloody all over.

After Toastie spotted Joe's Moving Carrot, the Harrington Corner Boys marched right up to Feisengrad and Joe. When they arrived alongside the shiny orange vehicle, they stepped back and looked it over admiringly. Then they receded like a web of elastic and snapped at the car, pushing their fists through the windshield, kicking in the doors, cracking the roof, and gouging the hood. They urinated on the brand new automobile as if it were a toilet.

Midge was wearing white shorts, red lipstick, white shoes, and a white halter-top. "You bastards!" Midge screamed. Her father took her by the arm, yanked her back inside the shop and pulled the shades down.

The Harrington Corner Boys were getting angrier as they ripped off the engine cover and smashed the valves and pistons into pieces on Gold Street. They didn't look at Midge.

If they did, it would have stopped them in their tracks. No one called a Cop, and no Umpire arrived to call this behavior SAFE or OUT.

Feisengrad remembered what his grandmother told him when he was born on Monday. She had said, "When you see the Sneezes, run the other way." He and Joe ran up Gold Street.

After the VDCs had their dinner (just southern vegetable), Feisengrad went to his room, his heart pounding, and stared at the sepia-colored wallpaper. The design was based on events from the Great Z Wars. There were tanks, jeeps, and fighter planes pictured in the searing heat of battle, and he wondered why he never studied the walls before. Everything comes in its own time, and now meant the rapid accumulation of images, ideas, and fear.

If his parents knew what happened at the Square, they would never allow him to leave. He realized that when he tried to sleep, his eyes would not close. The fear generated by the encounter was something he couldn't live with, awake or asleep. Who were these freaks, the Sneezes, who hated the Coughs? Although he was not a religious, dedicated Cough and didn't know anything about his religion, he was not going to accept what had happened. The memory of running away, retreating back up Gold Street disgusted him. The cowardly picture tossed around in his head like a small, white sailboat boat on a stormy, black sea.

There was a solution. He was going to challenge the Harrington Corner Boys. When he looked out the window and saw a full moon, he came to a conclusion—do or die! Many others had said the same words under the same circumstances, and he stepped into those classic old shoes the way his father dressed in battle fatigues. Planets and the horizon always helped when it came to making decisions, as long as one was able to stare at these images for long periods of time. No one had ever been to those places (especially the horizon), but whatever was out there was full of meaning or full of shit. In his mind, the moon was saying, "Go forth and protect what you are and what you stand for, otherwise you will lead a life of shame."

The moon wasn't actually saying anything, and all plow7s who received such profound messages later discovered the revelation or vibe meant the opposite of what it seemed to mean or nothing at all. These experiences were disappointing and soon forgotten until the next time a plow7 needed inspiration.

It was very important to trash bad memories and recall what was good about life in The Z. Right now, Feisengrad had to rid himself of what just happened at the Square.

The last thing he was going to do was tell his parents. He called up the drugstore and was channeled through the prescription line to the pharmacist.

"Is Toastie outside? I want to have a word with him," he axed.

"Are you a doctor?"

"No, I am Feisengrad, a Cough, and I don't have a cold. You don't know me. I just want to speak to Toastie. "

"He's outside repeatedly making an obscene gesture with his middle finger, so he might be very busy," the pharmacist replied and put the phone down quietly. The pharmacist opened the door a crack and axed Toastie to come to the phone.

"Who dat?" Toastie growled into the phone. He was so loud that the hairs on Feisengrad's feet twitched.

"I am Feisengrad. No Z cut for me. I live on Dirt Road, and you and the Harrington Corner Boys are challenged to a fight."

"A what? You mean a rumble? Are you kidding me? You stupid little Cough! We will beat da living shit outtayou. Hosty Toastie!" he snarled into the phone's mouthpiece. He ended every sentence with "Hosty Toastie." Many plow7s had silly sayings that meant absolutely nothing. Nonsense was nonsense and part of Z life.

"Midnight," was all Feisengrad said, and the phone line

went dead. He felt a burning rush in his chest, similar to his feelings for Grot, and wished he hadn't made the call. Fear is painful.

Like all heroes, he suffered from the intimidation that accompanies great accomplishment sometimes manifested by uncontrolled streams of urine discharged into his Riggs. The course of his life was irreversible. Could he phone the drugstore to say that it was all a horrible mistake? Would he get a recording axing him if he was a doctor? A wrong number, perhaps? Please ax Toastie not to take me seriously. I am barely three days old.

The fear didn't pass. It stayed right there, a rocky lump inside a small pillow. His parents were talking in the other room about paying the light bill, whether Feisengrad would ever get another job, and just who were his new friends?

If there was ever a time to find out if he had friends, this was it. It was the moment for Feisengrad to call them up. But he would need friends of friends and friends of those friends to take on the Harrington Corner Boys. He called up Joe Perfect, who was at home playing gin rummy with his father.

"I will get ready when this hand is finished. My hair never looked better," Joe Perfect told Feisengrad. He burped into the queen of spades, spread his winning cards on the table and exclaimed, "Gin," to his father.

"You better go down to the Square and kick ass and fuck them and their Z cuts," Joe Perfect's father grimaced and farted loudly, adding, "Don't you let this happen again to us Coughs."

"We have to pledge our lives to one another, Feisengrad. We have to stand tall and fight side-by-side and back-to-back like brothers. Before the fight, you and I will be blood brothers. I'll bring my blade, and our blood will flow together. If they cut you, I will bleed. I will bring all my cousins and uncles who are Coughs to the Square at midnight," Joe Perfect said.

Feisengrad telephoned Joe College. They hadn't spoken since the party on Power Drive, but there was a good feeling between them.

Joe College was at home, already in a brawl with his soldier brother, Magneto, who was home from one of the Great Z Wars for a day of rest and relaxation before returning to the front lines—wherever they then were. Joe College had expressed his opinion that there were possibly no Great Z Wars and no lines between the enemy and The Z Board. That made Magneto very angry. This was a very collegiate attitude, even though there were no colleges in The Z.

Most of the time, Magneto was supposedly far away from Gold Street, commanding troops to fight against anyone who wanted to change anything (at all) about The Z, but he could have been around the corner making a war movie. He told men in uniform to spit shine their boots, clean their rifles, do push-ups, clean the barracks, and run in place. When Magneto arrived at the College flat on Gold Street on Wednesday, he removed his hat and displayed his shiny brass medals and skirmish ribbons embedded in his pressed uniform. He looked like one of the Z movie stars.

Joe and Magneto argued about real blood and guts. They fought for hours until they were exhausted. Now there was another fight on the horizon. Some plow7s said that life was one long fight with short rounds in between, and no one was ever declared the winner.

If someone won a fight, he might be called a loser because he beat his wife or his wife was a drunk. Very often, the loser was considered the winner, because his wife was not a drunk, and he was known for not beating her. When Feisengrad called, Magneto had Joe College in a nasty headlock. He was choking and about to pass out. The two of them agreed to be at the Square at midnight.

Then there was Joe Blow. He was at home on Gold Street with his parents. They heard about the incident with the Harrington Corner Boys and The Z Cut. He put on a steel jockstrap, stuffed a monkey wrench in his back pocket and blew his nose into his hand, thinking it was going to be broken anyway a few hours from now. The Sneezes would want to break every Cough's nose. The Sneezes were very involved in religious imagery and ornament. Such specific acts of cosmetic violence were thought to purify The Z and were a giant leap toward having uniform noses.

Joe Blow felt good stuffing his baseball bat into a burlap bag for the fight at the Square. His father, Bosch Blow, said,

"Don't worry. The Harrington Corner Boys are not as tough as they say they are. You'll whip their asses." Plow7s always told other plow7s not to worry, which didn't mean anything.

His "don't worry" analysis didn't bring to mind the concept of victory any more than it conjured a picture of a whip snapping in the air over a group of stark naked asses. "Whip ass," "cream the motherfuckers," "beat shit," "fucking kill" maybe those expressions were all thought up by the same plow7... Before Joe Blow left, he called his cousin Lubovitch, once a professional boxer, who claimed, "I only fight for the pure beauty of the sport. It is Cough aesthetic." He, too, would be at the Square.

"Men, I would love to go with you. I remember when I was your age. It is a duty and an honor to defend the integrity of the Coughs," Joe Blow's father announced before leaving the room.

"And don't forget to be home by Thursday morning!" he yelled to his son as the door closed.

The moon was shining, reflecting off all the windows in The Z and giving off a sickly, milk-colored light. It made all the plow7s on Gold Street and Dirt Road wonder if the moon was sticky and was going to infect all them with an incurable disease. Something was going to happen. Would it be terrible? Would they be able to forget about it in just a few days?

Whenever a bad thing was going to happen, plow7s calculated the time it would take for the pain to pass. The plow7s had questions and wanted answers: "When will we be over it?" or "When could we put it behind us?" The full moon was not going to help anyone from worrying. "Shit! It is a full moon," could be heard all around The Z.

The letter to Grot was nearly done. When he finished writing, Feisengrad put his fountain pen down and thought about her. It was in moments like these that one indulged in reflection about mortality and how much one would be missed if one died. Mortality was the enemy of the plow7s, as well as the Umpires and Cops. It was the end of the line, and they all knew it was approaching like the tortoise that would win the race. The day was coming when all the fun and games of The Z would be total blackness—over. Moments before the last second of life, plow7s would look back, as if what they saw was a collage of smoldering, burnt metal as far as one could see. No streets, no Speedway, no sky. They would ax themselves, "What was that? Was it my life? How did that happen?" There would be questions, no answers, then blackness.

A poem? That might be the way to go. If I write her a poem, she will know how deeply I feel about her, and she will take me seriously. In The Z, flowers, poems, a box of sweet-tasting western vegetable or a bottle of perfume would make a woman feel attracted to the man who sent it to her. Opening a box with a gift inside caused cold bumps to form on a plow7's skin.

Perfume or flowers? They were out of the question. One couldn't even deliver them to Power Drive. There was no way to get inside, and you'd have to wait for a PDP to come out of there to get in—that meant being at the right place at the right time. A poem? That was another story. Poems could be sent through the mail, so long as you wrote on the outside of the envelope, "Poem Enclosed." So he decided to write a poem:

You were to be my girl but
now I am in the crusty mud,
looking for the light of day.

Standing on the edge of a cliff
waiting for God to appear.

And there he was
wearing a trench coat,
the wind whipping
its collar back.

He couldn't light his cigarette,
so I struck a match and
handed it to him,
but he pulled back and
disintegrated into
little scraps of paper.

They flew away

except for one small piece
the size of my thumb.

It had your name on it and
then it was gone too.

After he read it over twice, he was satisfied that it said
all the necessary things about love. He mailed it to "Grot,
Power Drive."

The temperature in The Z dropped sharply. It was much
lower than cool. Feisengrad headed for the Square. There was
no way for him to understand being a Cough. It was just a
group, and he had to meet the first obligation of being in it—to
protect what it stood for (whatever that was). Groups always
caused more trouble in The Z than individuals. It was safer to
be alone, especially at a time like this.

Now he was going off to war with his so-called "friends,"
and he would be dealing with loyalty, sacrifice, and altruism—
all the things his grandmothers desperately feared. Suddenly,
in a matter of minutes, these things were unavoidable. It was a
relief that they were dead and would not have to die again. All
generations have to be tested, and this was his test. It was the
same fight again and again but with different names and places.

Before he left, he called Cromwell, who said that he had
planned to go fishing—there were no fish in The Z—but he
would cancel because there was no way that the Sneezes were

going to beat up on the Coughs.

"Count me in, Feisengrad," Cromwell said. "Don't get the wrong idea. It was your idea to chase after that Sneezey girlfriend, Grot. I wouldn't be surprised if she called those Harrington Corner dogs down on you. Did you ever think about her being jealous of Midge?"

"I wasn't after Midge; Joe College was. I was just along for the ride."

"It was on your mind. Girls have a way of picking up on those thoughts," Cromwell laughed. "Don't worry, everyone wants to get it on with Midge."

Feisengrad arrived at the Square at eleven o'clock. It was empty and brightly lit as usual. There were no places to go anywhere in The Z that were not well-lighted, because all the plow7s were being filmed whenever they left their Opposite Houses or tenements. One wondered who had the time to look at all the footage, yet The Z Board seemed to be on top of it.

Whenever anyone committed a violation of the law, The Z Board promptly telecast that "show" on Z television as a form of entertainment. These shows were called crime shows, and the culprits were televised with their arms twisted up behind their backs saying things like, "Don't hurt me," or "Let me go, you son of a bitch."

The plow7s watched them, thinking about the serious consequences of misbehaving in The Z. Some plow7s were inspired by what they saw and mimicked the crime; these plow7s were labeled criminals. If they were caught, they were imprinted with the O. These "criminals" said that if they had not seen the crimes acted out on television, they would not have learned about crime.

It was the fault of The Z Board for creating these blueprints and shoving them down the plow7s' throats. Therefore, these criminals "didn't do nothin' wrong."

Again, Feisengrad paused on the sidewalk. No one. This is not possible; it is not how life works in The Z. There is always someone to fight with anytime, day or night, he thought.

Out of nowhere, there was a roar and harsh flashing lights sprung up. The Square was lit up as if a red sun was just miles down the road. Someone later said it was at that moment that all the plow7s' feet in The Z turned icy cold. There were Moving Carrots racing around the Square, honking their horns, their drivers screaming loudly, "Kill the Coughs! Kill the Coughs! Z cut them!" It was the Harrington Corner Boys, and they were arriving in droves, lining up their Moving Carrots in front of the Very Dry Cleaner in a long neat row.

On the other side of the Square, Feisengrad saw his friends Cromwell, Joe Perfect, Joe Blow, and Joe College. Lubovitch wore a blue sweat suit and air boxed. He threw light jabs into imaginary targets, forced air out of his nostrils and grunted. His lonely shadowy figure moved in an imaginary circle against the brightly lit drugstore sign.

WEDNESDAY'S MIDNIGHT

The clock was fixed on midnight. Feisengrad moved along the sidewalk, reviewing his troops—the ones he trained on the telephone two hours ago. Across the Square, Feisengrad saw Toastie punching himself in the thigh. His brother, Cronin, was smashing his forearm into the steering wheel of his Moving Carrot.

Then the Cops arrived and lifted the rope that stretched across the Square. No one knew why the Cops were there or why there was even a rope stretched across the Square. The Harrington Corner Boys drove toward Feisengrad. They wasted no time. Toastie pulled Joe College into his Moving Carrot and didn't let him out, beating his head against the dashboard. There was so much blood smeared on the windshield that you could not see inside.

Joe Blow smashed his wrench against the side of Cronin's skull, but it just bounced off. Cronin choked Joe Blow until his face turned bright pink, and he passed out. Then, Cronin

The Fight at the Square

carved his hair into a Z cut. Cronin's fist seemed to go right through Joe Blow's head, as he lay motionless on the ground.

"C'mon, it's my turn!" Lubovitch screamed to Toastie, as he threw some more fists into Wednesday night. Before Lubovitch knew what hit him, he was down on the ground with blood pouring out of his head. While Cronin crowned him with Joe Blow's wrench, Toastie broke Lubovitch's jaw with a straight right fist. Toastie knew something about the fine art of boxing, but he did not play by the formal rules and failed to retreat to his neutral corner. Instead, he repeatedly kicked Lubovitch in the chest and head until his eyes closed. Then he rolled Lubovitch into the Square's gutter.

In the meantime, Cromwell tried to escape from the Square, but one of the Harrington Corner Boys grabbed him by the back of his shirt and dragged him all the way back to the drugstore. Toastie was waiting. He picked Cromwell up with both hands, hoisted him over his head and threw him through the plate glass window that read in large white letters "Prescriptions Filled Here."

The Cops stood by with their arms folded across their chests and did nothing to stop the one-sided fight.

Feisengrad and Joe Perfect were the only ones left, and they stood back-to-back in the center of the Square while Toastie and the Harrington Corner Boys circled. Then the forces of nature struck.

One fist, followed by a bottle, the wrench, and then a

pipe sailed into Feisengrad and Joe. It was a mathematical transaction of violence—calculating, multiplying and then subtracting Feisengrad and his friends from The Z. Feisengrad's blood spilled, like it was poured from a large beaker, onto the sidewalk. It was just blood squared. Blood had been let so many times before in the Square that it was just another transaction of minds moving numbers to zero.

They threw the Coughs' bodies down to the asphalt, turned them into fractions and then to zeros. The Cops did nothing.

Then there was Toastie, triumphant, as he stepped on the broken and maimed numbers in the Square, the sidewalk, and the gutter. They had had their day, like some ancient battle fought with donkey jawbones; the Coughs that had showed lay piled in defeat, all with Z Cuts, next to where Lubovitch's dancing feet had made their last moves.

Feisengrad was dead. Toastie's fist cracked his temple straight into Feisengrad's last poem:

> The tall business-like undertaker
> was dressed to kill.

> He pulled open the door
> of the funeral parlor and
> stood on the porch.

> His shadow cast over the

newly planted front lawn.
He hated anything that
was crooked,
including the Park Here sign.
It was not parallel to the ground.

He decided to leave it alone,
because things would never
be right.

But it was only Wednesday, and tomorrow would be another
day, Thursday, and the week always ended on Sunday.

ABOUT THE AUTHOR

Aaron Richard Golub is a good man who may be the author of this small volume. As a boy, he lived on Gold Street before moving to an Opposite House on Dirt Road not far from where Feisengrad resided with his family. He was the first person to observe Feisengrad and follow his life pursuits until—

5753941R0

Made in the USA
Charleston, SC
29 July 2010